Death Plays a Part

Lesley Cookman

Published by Accent Press Ltd 2015

ISBN 9781521874677

Chapter One

May 1907

'That,' said Dorinda Alexander, 'is not what a fairy looks like.'

The fairy drooped. Dorinda – Dolly to her friends – stood with hands on hips considering her.

'Maude,' she said to the comfortable- looking woman standing next to her, 'what can we do about this?'

Maude crossed her arms under her ample bosom and frowned.

'I don't rightly know, Dolly. There wasn't no call for fairy costumes when we was The Wanderers.'

Dorinda stifled an impatient sigh. 'Of course not, Maudie. The Wanderers were Pierrots. But remember that you made me a costume overnight? When I needed it?'

Maude shrugged and smiled. 'Pierrots was easy. I'm not such a hand at anything else.'

Dorinda nodded. 'I know. I'm just grateful you've helped me as much as you have.' She turned to the fairy. 'Go and take it off, dear, and tell the others I won't need them until after lunch.'

'Couldn't you,' said Maude, as she followed Dorinda to the back of the sparkling new pavilion, 'just carry on with the Serenaders for a while? Until you've had a chance to sort of – look around a bit?'

Dorinda turned and looked back at the stage where men up ladders were painting large backcloths.

'That's just it, Maude. The Silver Serenaders have been great for me – for all of us – after all they got me this pitch

1

and now the pavilion.'

'With Sir Fred's help,' said Maude.

'Well, of course with his help.' Dorinda looked uncomfortable for a moment. 'But I want something different now. Look at all the shows that are going on in other places. Pierrots are on the way out. It's concert parties now, Maude.'

'Yes, Dolly,' said Maude, sighing.

Dorinda made her way back to her office thinking hard. The fairy number was not going to work if her chorus girls didn't look ethereal and sparkly. When she'd seen it performed in London the girls had drifted across the stage – almost appearing to float. Of course, the Gaiety Girls were the best in the business and the money spent on staging and costuming were out of her league, but she was determined to bring something of the London sophistication to Nethergate.

Ted and Algy fitted in well as the company comedians, and Will Beddowes, Maude's husband and founder of Nethergate's original Pierrots, Will's Wanderers. Will was still a good performer, but the girls were a different matter.

The Silver Serenaders had been formed by Dorinda from Will's Wanderers when Will himself had been seduced away by one of the big companies in the north-east. He had come back at the end of the season full of stories of the concert parties, and Dorinda, the first woman to run a company of Pierrots in a seaside town, had begun to think. The Serenaders were so successful after their first two seasons, largely due to Dorinda's decision to bring in girls as well as men that she was able to purchase her pitch under the cliff rather than pay the increased rent the council was demanding. From there it was a short step to deciding to build a pavilion, her beloved new Alexandria. After all, she reasoned, Will Caitlin in Scarborough had built his Arcadia, and other pavilions and theatres were appearing in seaside resorts up and down the country, on beaches, promenades and piers.

Dorinda had gone up to London to see some of the new Musical Comedies and come back inspired. This is what seaside entertainment should be, she thought, something new for the new century. There was a new King on the throne – why not new entertainment for the holiday makers?

Will, Ted and Algy had not been keen. Partly, she thought, because there were limited opportunities for them in this new format, but also because the seaside audiences loved what they were used to – comedy routines and Music Hall songs with which they could sing along. Yes, said Ted, put it undercover – they always lost several audiences to the weather – but keep it the same.

'When they start singing songs from the musicals on the streets, girl,' said Will, 'then you can bring them to the beach.'

So it was a compromise that Dorinda was rehearsing now. Sketches – some familiar, some new – a couple of solos and some set pieces. Besides, she thought, she didn't have an orchestra, only herself playing the piano, and the big musical comedy numbers wouldn't work so well with only piano accompaniment.

Her thoughts were interrupted by a knock on the door.

'Come in.'

A woman entered, tall, dark and fashionably, if quietly, dressed.

'Can I help you?' asked Dorinda, rising from her chair behind her desk.

'Er – I'm not sure.' The voice was pleasant, but hesitant. 'I think this is rather a cheek.'

Dorinda smiled and sat down. 'Take a seat,' she said. 'What can I do for you?'

Colour rose quickly above the woman's high collar. 'I – I – I just wondered … '

'Wondered what?'

3

'If you were looking for any singers.' The words came out in a rush.

'Oh!' Dorinda was surprised. She herself had approached some girls in London, mostly from the Music Halls like Collins in Islington, but it was rare that anyone approached her, unless introduced by another member of the company.

'I – er – heard you were taking on young ladies …' The woman stumbled to a halt.

'I am,' said Dorinda, now amused. 'Is that so unusual?'

'Oh, yes,' said the woman with certainty. 'Oh – I'm sorry!'

'Don't worry,' said Dorinda. 'Where did you hear this?'

'In London.' The young woman's dark eyes were now fixed on Dorinda like a mesmerised rabbit in front of a snake.

'London, eh? Were you working there?'

'I –' The woman stopped. 'Yes,' she said finally.

Something wrong there, thought Dorinda. The girl could be no more than twenty-five. Was she in trouble? Dorinda allowed her glance to travel down in search of a tell-tale bump under the skirt. There was none. She decided to take a chance.

'So you sing? What do you sing?'

'Anything.'

'"Ta-ra-ra Boom-de-ay?"'

The colour washed into the young woman's face again. 'Well, yes – I mean – I know it …'

'Off you go then,' said Dorinda, and sat back in her chair.

The woman stood up, pulled down the bottom of her little jacket and took a deep breath.

To Dorinda's astonishment, out came a very passable imitation of Lottie Collins' famous song that had captured London audiences a decade earlier. After two verses,

4

Dorinda signalled that she should stop.

'I'm not dressed for the dance, Miss Alexander, but I can actually perform that.' The woman sat down again.

'Well, well,' said Dorinda. 'And how about "A Bird In A Gilded Cage"?'

In total contrast to the previous song, the surprising woman began to sing the sentimental ballad perfectly.

'Not bad at all. What's your name?' asked Dorinda when the song had finished.

'Velda Turner.'

'Unusual name. Good for the halls,' said Dorinda. 'If you've been working in London, are you prepared to move to Nethergate?'

'Oh, yes,' said Velda. 'I'd like to.'

'Very well.' Dorinda stood up. 'You can start straight away. I'll take you round the back to meet the others after lunch. Can you be back here for two o'clock?'

Velda looked lost for a moment. 'Yes ... yes, of course,' she said, and stood up. Dorinda watched her go out of the office and felt guilty. The poor woman probably hadn't got anywhere to go for the next hour, but Dorinda did not want to spend it babysitting the new recruit. She had fairies to dress.

An hour later, sitting on the edge of the stage in a sea of pink gauze, Dorinda had almost forgotten Velda, until the young woman appeared hesitantly at the back of the hall. Maude raised her eyebrows. Dorinda slid off the stage and went forward to lead the newcomer onto the stage.

As she introduced Velda to the other girls in the chorus she was aware of a slight feeling of hostility, especially from the bold and brash Aramantha Giles, the aspiring soubrette. Dorinda was pretty sure her real name was nothing like Aramantha, but if that's what she chose to call herself, that was all right with Dorinda, who had changed her own name, albeit the other way round. Dolly was a far better name for a concert party performer than Dorinda, which had suited the prim and proper governess she had been before her transformation.

'Where d'yer work, then?' Aramantha was asking – a touch condescendingly.

'The Britannia. Before, of course … '

'Before what?' asked one of the youngest girls, as the others all gasped.

'It burned down,' someone informed her. They all looked with new respect at Velda Turner. It belatedly occurred to Dorinda that she'd taken the girl on trust – hadn't asked where she'd worked, or even from whom in London she'd heard of Dorinda and the Alexandria. Mentally shaking herself, she broke into the conversation.

'Do you need help finding digs?'

'Ma Butcher's got room, if you don't mind sharing,' volunteered shy Maisie Birchall. 'If you need …' surprised by the sound of her own voice she looked round wildly, and Dorinda patted her shoulder.

'Well, yes, thank you, I do need!' Velda smiled at Maisie. 'Are you sure Mrs Butcher won't mind?'

'More money, innit?' said Aramantha, looking slightly disgruntled. 'Not sure I'd like to share, meself.'

The other girls exchanged knowing looks, and Dorinda laughed. 'Come on, girls, little birds in their nests agree! Now shall we run through the fairy number again? Velda can watch to get the hang of it first. Do you want to start straight away, Velda?'

'Yes, please.' Velda sat down on one of the new seats in the auditorium and Dorinda went to the piano.

The fairy song, a popular one lifted from one of Mr Edwardes' musical entertainments at The Gaiety in London didn't quite go as well as Dorinda wanted.

'Well,' she said with a sigh, when the girls had come to a ragged halt in a parody of their finishing positions. 'Perhaps the costumes will help. The pink tulle will be better than those peasant things.'

6

'Excuse me.' Velda appeared silently by Dorinda's left shoulder. 'Could a young lady perhaps take a solo in the song? I've seen it done like that, and the others are as still as statues while she sings it.'

Dorinda stared at her. 'You've seen it?'

'Yes.' Velda stepped back.

Dorinda regarded her solemnly for a moment. 'Go on, then. Go and arrange them and tell them what to do. Who do you think should sing the solo?'

Velda stepped on to the stage with alacrity and laid a hand on Aramantha's shoulder. 'This one.' Then under the astonished gaze of the company, including Dorinda and Maude, she proceeded to position Maisie and the other three girls around Aramantha in the middle and took a place herself.

'And we sing the choruses without moving a muscle,' she said.

'Except our mouths,' said Maisie, and they all giggled.

Velda nodded to Dorinda, and the number started. Dorinda couldn't believe the difference between the two performances. At the end, they were greeted with a burst of clapping from the back, and Will, Ted and Algy came down towards the stage.

'Superb!' said Ted. 'And who are you?'

Velda blushed and stepped back behind Aramantha.

'Well, who is she?' murmured Will to Dorinda. 'We came in as she was arranging them all, but we stayed quiet.'

'I've no idea,' said Dorinda. 'She came in asking for work and said she'd heard I was hiring in London. Worked at The Britannia, she says.'

'So where's she been since it burnt down?' Algy came up on her other side, while Ted remained on stage surrounded (as usual) by what Dorinda called his harem.

'I don't know. It looks as though she knows a lot more about the business than your average chorus girl, though, doesn't it?'

'What's her name?' asked Maude, suddenly appearing beside them. 'She's just given me an idea for that pink tulle. Just to sort of drape it on them. Says she's seen it done.'

'And she's seen the fairy song done ...' murmured Dorinda. 'Where have you come from, Velda Turner?'

'I think,' said Will, watching as Velda quietly left the stage and resumed her seat in the auditorium, 'that you'd better watch your Velda Turner.'

Chapter Two

The Alexandria opened its doors to the paying public five days later. The first of the wealthier families had already arrived to take the large houses for the summer, although the majority of the holiday makers, the 'Arries and 'Arriets, wouldn't start arriving yet, apart from the weekend visitors. Dorinda had made sure the company were seen in town, handing out the flyers that informed the public that The Silver Serenaders were still there, but now performing at the newly built Alexandria.

She'd given in over the costumes, and for the *ensemble* pieces allowed the old Pierrot costumes to be used. For two handers and solos, evening dress would be worn, and in the fairy song, Velda's innovative drapery of pink tulle. Unsurprisingly, this was the hit of the performance, so Dorinda moved it to close the first half of the programme. Luckily it was usual to provide programmes that gave rather indefinite lists of items, as the programme had to change at least once a week, and often more. Nethergate's holiday makers and temporary residents wanted to be entertained, but they didn't want to see exactly the same thing every time they visited.

Velda was proving to be a quiet, unassuming member of the company, yet able to carry off a solo performance with as much verve as a London music hall star. The only person who didn't appreciate this was Aramantha. Not that Dorinda worried that the girl might attempt to sabotage her new rival, but it had made for uncomfortable tensions backstage. Dorinda, out front with her piano, wasn't aware of this until it was reported to her by Maude.

'The other girls won't tell you,' she said. 'When you go behind in the interval they all shut up.'

And, indeed, this was what happened. Dorinda was careful not to make too much of Velda, although the girl had more talent than any of the others. Dorinda often found herself wondering again why Velda should have turned up here at a new pavilion theatre in the small town of Nethergate, when it was obvious that she could easily be making a name for herself on the halls. As, presumably, she had been at The Britannia. As Algy had said, where had she been since then? She was not as young as she first appeared, and Dorinda wondered if, in fact, she was a former music hall star down on her luck and trying to make a new name for herself. But no one had recognised her, not even the two girls who had been working in London before she enticed them to the seaside.

It was Saturday, changeover day. A day when The Serenaders, dressed in their silver Pierrot costumes, would gather at the railway station (and what a difference that had made to Nethergate's fortunes) to say goodbye to the last week's audience and be there to tell the newcomers about the shows. Of course, they weren't the only ones. Now Will's Wanderers and the Silver Serenaders were off the beach, the Magic Minstrels, led by Will Beddowes' old rival Mickey Bennett, had taken up residence further along towards the little harbour. Mickey had finally eschewed the traditional black face of the minstrels, and opted for smart white trousers, blazers and boaters for his six man troupe, but still used the traditional format of sitting in a line and using the cross talk act, kept in line by "Mr Interlocutor", in this case, Mickey himself. He was inclined to favour Dorinda and her Alexandria, on the basis that his audience could be everyone, while Dorinda's had to pay up front. Mickey's bottler, a young boy with deceptively innocent large brown eyes was able to prise a good deal of money from a crowd as he went round shaking the box – or "bottle" – in front of them. Ladies, in particular were susceptible to those eyes, he found – and so did Mickey.

Dorinda, in a formal grey walking costume, watched her company from Victoria Place as they returned from the station.

'What are they like?' she asked as Ted and Algy came to a halt beside her.

'Not bad. Some from last year,' said Algy.

'What did they say about the pavilion?'

'Looked a bit doubtful, some of them,' said Ted. 'Thought it might be too posh!'

'Oh, dear.' Dorinda sighed. She had feared this. .

'We told 'em it was the same old rubbish, though!' laughed Algy.

'Algy!' Ted nudged his friend. 'Sorry, Dolly.'

Dorinda laughed. 'Well, it is the same old rubbish! Until we can afford to pay for some new songs.'

'And new gags,' said Ted. 'I'm sure Mickey Bennett's using the same ones we are at the other end of the beach.'

'That Velda's got some good ideas, though,' said Algy.

'I thought you warned me to keep an eye on her?' said Dorinda, turning to walk down to The Alexandria.

'Well, yes, I think you should.' Algy pondered, staring out to see, his long lugubrious face thoughtful. 'Not quite like the rest of us, is she?'

'Bit too classy?' said Ted with a grin.

'Well … not exactly. But then again … '

'She *has* got class,' said Dorinda, opening the doors of The Alexandria. 'Rather more than the rest of us.'

'Except you,' said Algy.

'Hmm.' Dorinda opened the door to her office and stopped so suddenly that Algy and Ted cannoned into her.

'What the –?' Algy gasped.

'Gawd!' said Ted.

The office was a mess. Paper was strewn everywhere,

ink had been sprayed over every surface and there was an ominous smell coming from near the window.

Ted pushed Dorinda aside and made his way through the debris. By the window he bent and picked something up. Dorinda's hand flew to her mouth as he straightened up holding a very dead and somewhat ravaged seagull.

'Go on, girl,' he said, 'you go and get a cuppa. Algy and me'll clear up here. Anything we didn't ought to see?'

Too shocked to speak, Dorinda shook her head and went back into the foyer, where Maude found her a few minutes later.

'Deliberate, it was, then,' said Maude, after Dorinda had described the scene. Will had appeared while she was talking and been sent summarily to help Ted and Algy.

'I don't think the dead seagull did it,' said Dorinda with a tremulous laugh. She realised she was shaking. 'Come on, Maude. Let's go and make that cup of tea.'

Tucked away backstage Dorinda had managed to incorporate a tiny little stove, for the company to make tea, or boil up little messes of whatever they could get hold of to eat between shows. There wasn't always enough time to get a proper meal, and there wasn't always enough money to pay for them.

The girls dribbled in, Maisie and Velda last, and Maude told them what had happened.

''Oo done it, then?' asked Aramantha. 'And why?'

'I've no idea,' said Dorinda. 'As it happens, it hasn't done us any real harm. We can still go on. It's not as if it was the costumes or the piano, is it?'

'You sure?' Phoebe, a dark, pessimistic girl with a sigh like the hopeless north wind, shook her head.

'I've checked,' said Maude, 'and Will, Algy and Ted are going round the rest of the place now to make sure.'

Inspection of the pavilion complete, the company gathered on stage.

'No other damage,' reported Will. 'We piled up all the

12

papers best we could, Dolly, but that ink'll have to be scrubbed off the walls.'

'So, who's got a grudge against us?' asked Ted. 'That's what it looks like, don't it?'

'Mickey Bennett?' suggested Maude.

Dorinda, Will and Ted shook their heads. 'No, we're good for him,' said Will. 'Healthy competition.'

', Stet Doll?' asked Algy. 'What about that builder you turned down?'

The girls looked up, interested. They weren't here in the winter.

'He quoted too much money,' Dorinda told them. 'I think he was just lazy and didn't want the job.'

'What about the builder who did do the job?' asked Velda.

'He was good,' said Will, and Ted and Algy nodded. 'Got the job done quick, no skimping. We mucked in, too. And he was paid right on time, too. Nothing there.'

'Who else, then?' asked Maude. 'Someone you didn't hire?'

Dorinda frowned. 'No, no one. I didn't advertise. I went up to London myself and recruited Phoebe and Aramantha, and Maisie, Patsy and Betty were already here.'

'What about that pianist who auditioned? He wanted to bring a fiddle in, didn't he?' said Algy.

'He wasn't very good, and anyway, I told him honestly that I couldn't afford to pay another pianist, let alone a violinist. I don't think he was upset..'

'So what, then?' said Aramantha. 'One o' them young lads 'oo 'ang about?'

'They'd have taken something. Nothing was taken, was it Will?'

'Don't think so, Doll. Was there anything to take, though?'

Dorinda shook her head. 'Nothing. No money on the

13

premises.'

'We better not leave the place empty,' said Maude.

'How do we manage that then?' asked Ted. 'Sleep here each night?'

Maude looked doubtfully at Dorinda. 'Well ... '

'No. We simply make sure it's locked up tight. Could you see how someone had got in?'

Will, Ted and Algy all shook their heads. 'But you hadn't locked the front doors.'

'No.' Dorinda sighed. 'I only popped up to the prom to see you come back. I was only gone oh – I don't know, fifteen or twenty minutes.'

'Tell the police, then?' asked Maude.

'That Constable Fowler isn't going to be much good, is he?' said Will. 'I've known Fred Fowler since he was a lad. Soft as butter, he is.'

'I think perhaps we should,' said Dorinda. 'Who was the policeman we met before?'

There was a sudden silence.

'When before?' asked Maisie.

'Oh, a couple of years ago,' said Dorinda eventually, when no one else seemed inclined to speak.

'What 'appened?' asked Aramantha, suspiciously.

'There was some trouble from a member of the audience,' said Will with a warning glance at Dorinda. 'We had to get him removed.'

'Retired, I reckon,' said Ted. 'That constable, I mean.'

'Of course,' said Dorinda. She cleared her throat. 'But I think we ought to tell Constable – Fowler, did you say, Will? In case anything else happens.'

Will nodded. 'I'll go before the next show. Better get out of this, though.' He indicated his costume.

'And you should all get something to eat, now,' said Dorinda. 'I'll make a start on cleaning this ink up.'

'That you won't,' said Maude. 'One of you girls get me a bucket of water – go on, Phoebe, that's right – and

14

Aramantha, find me a scrubbing brush – '

'I ain't no cleaner!' Aramantha screeched, and flounced back to the foyer.

'I'll go with Phoebe,' said Maisie.

'So will I,' said Velda.

'And me,' said Betsy, and Patty nodded, eyes wide.

Dorinda sat down on the edge of the stage, shoulders slumped. The men had all gone backstage to change out of their Pierrot costumes. Maude came and sat beside her.

'Nothing to do with that old business, is it?' she asked quietly.

'I can't see how it could be,' said Dorinda. 'It was all over and done with back then, and look how far we've come.'

'Not quite all over and done with,' said Maude.

'Well, no.' Dorinda looked uncomfortable.

'Anyway, makes sense to tell the police. Just in case.' Maude climbed down from the stage. 'I'll go and get scrubbing.'

Just before the afternoon show, Will put his head round the office door.

'Left a message with Fred Fowler's wife.' He shrugged. 'What good it'll do, I don't know.'

Dorinda stared out of the window. 'Neither do I,' she said.

Chapter Three

In between shows another train was due to arrive, courtesy of the South Eastern and Chatham Railway. Will took charge and sent Ted and Algy with Phoebe, Maisie, Patsy and Betty to meet any newcomers, while he and Maude sat with Dorinda in the office.

'You don't have to keep an eye on me,' said Dorinda, with a laugh, as she pulled off her Pierrot hat and let her hair fall down. 'No one's going to break in and attack me now, are they? Where are Velda and Aramantha?'

'Round the back,' said Maude. 'Aramantha's sulking and Velda's sewing something.'

'She's a strange one, isn't she?' said Dorinda. 'So quiet, yet so talented. I can't help thinking she doesn't belong here.'

'No more do you, duck,' said Maude. 'But here you are.'

Dorinda regarded her friend thoughtfully. 'Yes, here I am. Do you think perhaps Velda has something in her past …?'

'Could be.' Will stretched out his legs. 'Nowhere else to go, maybe.'

'Like me,' said Dorinda.

'Now, don't start,' said Maude.

'If you hadn't taken me in…' began Dorinda.

'Be quiet!' said Maude.

'You shut up, now, Dorinda Alexander,' said Will.

Dorinda smiled at them both. 'But I still don't know what I'd have done without you,' she said.

'And you repaid us, didn't you? Look at this lot.' Will

made a sweeping gesture to encompass the whole pavilion. 'There we was, one step up from the minstrels on the sands, not even a bit of shelter.'

'You were very popular,' said Dorinda. 'That's why we've still got a following now, even after we changed our name.'

'We could hardly be Will's Wanderers when Will wasn't there, could we?' said Maude.

'It worked out,' said Dorinda, getting to her feet. 'Now all we have to worry about is making enough to keep this place up.'

'And finding out who don't like us,' said Maude. 'I'll run and get a couple of pies, shall I?'

Constable Fred Fowler, uncomfortable in his helmet and tunic, turned up just before the evening show. Maude, selling tickets at the front, frowned at him.

'You can't talk to anyone now, Fred. They're just going on stage.'

'What am I going to do, then?' He looked helplessly at the audience, filing in to sit on the benches. There were only a couple of rows of the more comfortable seats at the front.

'Once they've started I'll show you Miss Alexander's office,' said Maude, smiling at two excited children with their parents. 'No, you just go and make yourself scarce for a bit or you'll scare off all these people.'

Fred slipped out and hid round the back of the new pavilion. At least it would give him the chance of a crafty pipe.

'Constable,' said a quiet voice in his ear.

Fred jumped.

'Gawd, sir!' He dropped his pipe.

The man raised his eyebrows. 'I was only saying good evening to a fellow smoker.' He waved a pipe.

'Ah. Aye, sir.' Fred re-lit his pipe watching the newcomer out of the corner of his eye.

'Not taking these lovely ladies and gents in charge, are you?' The man leant on the railing Dorinda had erected behind the pavilion to separate it from the beach.

'Ha – no, sir.' Fred laughed unconvincingly.

'Keeping an eye on the public, then? Pickpockets in the audience?'

Fred gulped. 'I hope not, sir.'

'Oh?' The man turned to look at him. Well dressed, Fred thought. Tweeds, though, not evening dress.

'Well sir –' he began.

'Fred Fowler! You come in here now.' Maude appeared round the corner of the building, arms akimbo, eyes fixed suspiciously on the stranger.

Fred hastily tipped his helmet to his new acquaintance and stuffed his pipe in his pocket.

'Who was that?' asked Maude, as she ushered him through the doors towards Dorinda's office.

'Dunno,' said Fred. 'Just a cove having a smoke.'

'Funny place to choose,' said Maude, opening the office door.

'Is it? I was there.'

'Because you were visiting the pavilion. What was he doing there?'

'I don't know, do I?' said Fred, exasperated.

'When you've come to look into a break in and there's a suspicious stranger hanging around, p'raps you should've found out.' Maude stood looking at him. 'Go on. Start looking.'

During the interval, Dorinda joined him in the office.

'Found anything, constable?'

'No, Miss.' Fred stood as she entered, having been sitting mournfully on the visitor's chair for the last half an hour. 'Nothing except the ink what Maude – beg pardon – Mrs Beddowes has took off.'

'What do we do then?' Dorinda flung herself down in her own chair and pulled off her hat. Fred's eyes bulged as

18

the luxuriant dark tawny hair tumbled out.

'Don't know, miss,' he stuttered. Pulling himself together, he straightened up. 'Nothing was took, Mrs Beddowes said.'

'Not as far as I could see.'

'Just lads, then? Making mischief.' He nodded, confident.

'Perhaps. I shall make sure The Alexandria is locked up tight whenever we're not here.' Dorinda looked at him, her head on one side. 'And you'll patrol here, will you? I know you patrol the sea front.'

Fred took off his helmet and wiped his forehead. 'As often as I can, Miss. There's only me, see.'

'I see.' Dorinda nodded. 'So you can't keep an eye on any suspicious newcomers all the time?'

'No, miss – there's too many newcomers every week. Although –' Fred stopped. 'There was this gentleman earlier. Behind the pavilion, he was.'

Dorinda sat up straight. 'Oh? Who was he? Why was he there?'

'He was just having a smoke, Miss, like me. I dunno who he was, Maude called me in before I could – er – ʼhascertain.' Fred produced the word with a certain triumph.

'You said "gentleman". Was he?'

'Seemed like it. Spoke nice. Polite.'

Dorinda frowned. 'Old? Young?'

'Not old, Miss. Not young, neither. Sort of middling.'

'Ted's age? Will's?'

'Younger, Miss. But not erzackly *young*, if you get my meaning.'

No one she knew, then, thought Dorinda. Just a holidaymaker having a smoke, as Constable Fowler said. She nodded.

'Very well, then constable. Thank you for your time and trouble. We'll try and make sure no one else gets in.'

Dorinda stood up. 'Now I'd better get back for the second half.' She paused. 'Would you like to sit in? I'm sure we can squeeze you into the back row – without your helmet of course.'

Fred Fowler blushed crimson and bowed. 'Thank you, Miss. Appreciate it, I'm sure.'

Dorinda bundled her hair up under hat again, checked her appearance in the flyblown mirror on her wall and followed Fred Fowler out of the office.

The second half went as well as the first, and when the audience had been sent happily into the night, vowing to return later in the week, Dorinda and her company gathered again on the stage.

'Well done everyone,' said Dorinda. 'The police are now aware of our break-in, and with any luck nothing else will happen.'

'Jealousy, I reckon,' said Aramantha. All the other girls nodded and murmured agreement. Dorinda looked gratified.

'You think so?' she said. 'If that's all it is then we should be flattered. Now, off you go and get a good night's sleep.'

'Fred said to tell you he enjoyed the show,' said Maude, as the others left the stage. 'And he'll keep an eye out for the gentleman.

'What gentleman?'

'He said he was talking to a gentleman behind the pavilion. Did you see who it was?'

'Did I! I told Fred off for not asking him his business. Funny place to be for a smoke, I said.'

'You didn't know who it was, then?'

'No. Couldn't barely see him – getting dark it was. Didn't look like a tough, though.'

'More toff than tough?' asked Dorinda with a grin.

'Get on with you!' Maude giggled.

The next morning Dorinda was at The Alexandria

early. Her lodgings, shared with Maude and Will, were comfortable and not too far from the seafront, so it was no hardship to get to the pavilion before nine o'clock. She unlocked carefully and began a tour through the premises. Everything was exactly as she had left it the previous night. To her surprise, she hadn't been in the office more than ten minutes when Constable Fowler put his head round the door.

'Morning, Miss! Saw the door open, so I thought I'd check.'

Dorinda smiled. 'Oh, Fred – I may call you Fred, mayn't I? – that's wonderful. I feel so much better knowing you're looking out for us.'

Fred blushed. 'Pleasure, Miss. Thought it was a lovely show last night. I'll have to bring the missis to see the whole thing when I get a night off.'

'You do that, Fred. On the house.'

Fred stuttered disclaimers and thanks all the way out the door, and Dorinda set about working out the change of programme for mid-week. It being Sunday, there were still trains to meet, as the day trippers would be coming, but the schedule was tighter, as the evening show would be earlier to accommodate those who had to travel back home, some as far as London.

The first to arrive was Velda, who also put her head round the door of the office.

'You're early,' said Dorinda. 'No Maisie?'

'Not yet, Miss Dorinda. She's only just got up. Mrs Butcher was shouting.'

'Oh, dear.' Dorinda laughed. 'Maisie in trouble again, is she?'

'No.' Velda gave a slight smile. 'It's just Mrs Butcher's way. Excuse me, Miss.'

Dorinda watched the girl disappear round the back of the stage. 'And I still don't know what to make of her,' she said to herself.

One by one, the company appeared, and by the time the last one, Aramantha, had deigned to put in an appearance, the first wave had already left to greet day trippers at the station.

'Do you think you could try to be here a little earlier, dear?' asked Dorinda, following her aspiring star through the auditorium. 'Especially when we need to meet the trippers.'

'I don't see why we have to meet 'em. See us 'ere, don't they.' Aramantha disappeared into the dressing room she shared with the other girls. Dorinda couldn't yet afford separate dressing rooms for principals, or the principals to put in them.

'We need to let them know we are here,' Dorinda patiently explained. 'We always do it. Did you not do it before?'

'No.' Aramantha didn't look at her, and Dorinda wondered again if the glowing references she had received from Aramantha's previous employers could possibly be forgeries. Only the girl's undoubted talent had convinced her to take her on.

Aramantha now turned to face her. 'Why don't you 'ave them postcards printed? Instead o' them flyers?'

'They're more expensive,' said Dorinda, although in truth, she had been thinking along those lines herself.

'Classier.' Aramantha turned back to the dressing table and hunched a shoulder. Dorinda felt herself dismissed.

She returned to her office and tried to concentrate on the new programme, but somehow, it wouldn't hold her attention. She turned instead to the window and gazed out at the sea on her right and the promenade on her left. The promenade, renamed Victoria Place, was now bright with flowers. Above it, little Cliff Terrace stood with its row of thin houses dating from the end of the eighteenth century. This was where she had first stayed in Nethergate. She shivered slightly and went to turn back to her desk when something caught her eye.

Leaning on the railings of Cliff Terrace, a young man was staring down at The Alexandria. Almost, Dorinda thought, as if he could see right through her window and into her eyes. She stepped back and narrowed her eyes to see him better. Tall, she thought. Brown suit? Dark hair. No moustache. And as she watched, she thought she saw him smile and raise the pipe he was holding in a mocking salute.

Chapter Four

'Maude!' Dorinda called. Her voice echoed round the empty pavilion.

She hovered in the foyer. Should she go out? Challenge the man? Find that he wasn't looking at, or gesturing to her but to some companion unseen?

The front doors rattled and Dorinda's heart jumped in her chest and she consciously smoothed out her expression.

'What's the matter, Doll?' Will stopped short as he came through the doors and Dorinda's heart jumped back down again.

'I thought ...' she began, and stopped. 'Oh, it sounds silly, Will. I've just got a bit unsettled by the business yesterday.'

Will took off his Pierrot hat and pushed a hand through his hair. 'I reckon it unsettled us all. Maude not here? Well, let's go back and make ourselves some tea on your little stove, shall we? Nothing like a nice cup of tea.'

'Aramantha's here. In the dressing room,' said Dorinda, following him through the auditorium.

'Wasn't her that scared you, was it?'

'No, of course not. And I wasn't scared ... just ...'

'Go on then, what was it?' Will led the way in to the area between the dressing rooms where the little pot-bellied stove stood and handed her the kettle. Dorinda took it to the sink.

'Yesterday, Constable Fowler met someone behind the building while he was waiting for the interval.'

'Met someone? Who?'

'Oh, not intentionally. He went to have a smoke, he says, and someone was already there. It seemed odd to me, somehow. A strange place for a smoke. And Maude came out to call him and told him he shouldn't have been talking to a stranger.'

'I don't know about that,' said Will, putting the kettle on the stove. 'Have to talk to strangers all the time here, don't we?'

'It was because of the break in. Any stranger could be suspicious.'

'And wouldn't still be hanging around half a day later,' said Will. 'So what was up this morning?'

'I thought I saw the same man up on Cliff Terrace. Watching the pavilion.'

Will's eyes widened. 'You saw him too?'

'Not yesterday. Constable Fowler described him.'

'Now, you couldn't know it was the same bloke, could you? Not for certain. Only Fred could.'

'Or Maude. She saw him. That was why I was calling her.'

'And she's not here? Where'd she go?'

'I think she went out with Betty and Patsy to the station. She had her hat on.'

Will frowned. 'She doesn't have to do that.'

'No, I've told her, but she likes to go. She only does it when you're not here,' said Dorinda with a mischievous smile.

'Be the death of me, she will,' said Will with an answering, if reluctant, smile.

'Of course she won't. She's the best wife anyone could ever want,' said Dorinda. 'Shall I make the tea?'

'Tea?' Aramantha appeared at the dressing room door. 'Go on, then. Don't mind if I do.'

Will and Dorinda exchanged looks.

'I'll just go and see if she's coming,' said Will and disappeared into the auditorium.

25

''E don't like me,' said Aramantha consideringly, watching his back.

'What makes you say that?' asked Dorinda, unable to refute the suggestion.

'None of 'em do.' Aramantha settled back in a chair, sounding unconcerned. 'You don't, neither.'

Dorinda turned to face her. 'Do you actually do anything to make us like you?'

Aramantha looked shocked. 'I never …'

'Never what?' Dorinda shook her head. 'You're rude to everyone, including me, and although I'll admit you're very good on stage, you aren't a generous performer, are you?'

'I dunno what you mean!' Aramantha snatched a cup of tea from Dorinda's hand and stood up. Calmly, Dorinda took the cup back.

'Yes, you do. And unless you want to find yourself out of a shop at the beginning of the season, you'd better start behaving.'

'And wot would you do wivout me?'

'Oh, we'd cope. You're no Marie Lloyd, you know.'

Dorinda waited to see what affect her words would have. In truth, Aramantha would leave a hole in the show, but sometimes it was better to have a happy company than a corrosive star turn.

The other girl stared at her for a moment, then went back into the dressing room. Dorinda sighed and poured more tea.

'Here, Dolly,' Maude came bustling through the auditorium followed by Will. 'Guess who I've just seen?'

'The man Fred saw yesterday?' suggested Dorinda.

'Oh – yes.' Maude was deflated. 'How d'you know?'

'I thought I saw him up on Cliff Terrace a little while ago. He seemed to be looking at The Alexandria.'

'That's exactly what I thought!' Maude was triumphant. 'I saw him there as I was coming back from

26

the station, so I goes up to him and I says: "If you're looking for some real entertainment sir, that's the place for it. Our Alexandria." And I gave him a leaflet.'

'And what did he say?' Dorinda didn't try to hide her amusement.

'Thank you very much, if you please. Nothing else!'

Will laughed. 'And he's still there!'

Dorinda looked from one to the other. 'Should I go and speak to him, do you think?'

'Why?' said Will. 'He's spoken to Fred, and now Maude, and he seems to be keeping an eye on us. If he wants anything else, he can come and ask, can't he?'

Dorinda shrugged. 'It can't be a secret, so it can't be dangerous.' She paused. 'Unless it's the bailiffs!'

'You aren't in debt, girl,' said Maude. 'How could it be the bailiffs?'

'Someone in the company?' said Dorinda. 'I wouldn't have thought so, but we don't know the girls well, do we? Not all of them.'

'We know Maisie, Betty and Patsy,' said Maude. 'They were with us last season. It wouldn't be them.'

Dorinda cast an apprehensive look at the dressing room door and, handing them each a cup, drew them away into the auditorium, where she told them of her altercation with Aramantha.

'Well, you can't say she doesn't deserve it,' said Will. 'Trouble is, she's a good little performer.'

'Pinches the limelight,' said Maude. 'She elbowed young Maisie practically off the platform the other night.' Maude was still having trouble with coming to terms with the word "stage."

'We'll see how things are today,' said Dorinda. 'She might walk out on us.'

'She's got more sense. You pointed out that she wouldn't have a shop.'

'She'd find one easily enough if she went round some

of the other resorts,' said Maude.

'But she'd have nowhere to live and no money,' said Will. 'She'd be better staying here.'

It appeared that Aramantha agreed, for she joined the company in good time for the first show and was uncharacteristically quiet. She didn't attempt to upstage any of the other girls, and even when they were wearing their own evening dresses, she had played down her usual flamboyance. Dorinda kept an eye on her all afternoon, but Aramantha didn't put a foot wrong.

'Well,' she said to Will and Maude later in the office, 'I don't know what exactly hit the spot, but she was a lot better, wasn't she?'

'Although the husbands in the audience didn't get as much of an eyeful as they usually do,' said Will with a laugh.

'In that case the wives might let them out to come to the midweek show,' said Maude.

'By which time Aramantha will probably be back to normal,' said Dorinda. 'But let's hope not *too* normal.'

To everyone's surprise, however, the following day, when Dorinda suggested a stroll along the promenade in costume to hand out leaflets to those holidaymakers who'd been fortunate enough to dodge them the previous day, Aramantha agreed quite happily and set off with Phoebe, Betty, Ted and Dorinda, while Algy collected Velda, Maisie, Patsy and Will. Maude stayed behind in case a stray customer should wander in wanting tickets.

Dorinda was still shy when faced with the public, so stayed in the background, but she had to admit that between them, Ted and Aramantha did a wonderful job of charming their potential audience. Phoebe, Betty and she had little more to do than hover in the background smiling hopefully. At one point, just where the old bandstand stood beyond Cliff Terrace, they collected such a crowd that the three of them retreated to the low stone wall bordering the flowerbeds and sat down.

'Don't know what we bothered to come out for,' said Phoebe.

'Because five of us together, all in costume, is a more striking picture,' said Dorinda.

''S'pose,' said Phoebe, staring gloomily at the crowd round her fellow performers.

Aramantha obviously decided then that enough was enough, and waving gaily to her admirers, began to turn back towards The Alexandria. Phoebe, Betty and Dorinda jumped off the wall and fell in behind.

They were almost back at the pavilion when Dorinda saw him. Still in the brown suit, still leaning on the railings, still raising his pipe in acknowledgement. She turned to Phoebe and Betty.

'See that man there? In the brown suit without a hat.'

Phoebe nodded and Betty looked interested.

'Have you ever seen him before?'

'No, who is he?' asked Betty.

'I don't know, but he's been asking questions about us.' Dorinda frowned and turned to go down the slope to The Alexandria.

'What, you mean the Serenaders?' said Betty.

'I'm not sure if it's the company or … well, or what. But he was around after our break in. I don't like it.'

'Oh, I don't know,' said Betty. 'I think he looks lovely.'

Dorinda gave her a warning look. 'Don't you go talking to him, miss!'

'I could find out all about him.' Betty tried to peer round Dorinda.

'I don't want to know,' said Dorinda pushing open the door into the foyer.

'He's there again,' said Maude, appearing from the office.

'I know.' Dorinda sighed.

29

Will came through the auditorium. 'He spoke to me as we went past.'

'What? What did he say?'

'Just – "business good, then?" That was it.'

'Go on, girls, go and get ready for the first show,' said Dorinda. 'So what's he doing?' she continued to Will. 'Is he something to do with yesterday? Is he watching us for someone else? And if so, who?'

'There's one simple way to find out,' said Maude. 'Go and ask him.'

Dorinda stopped in the act of taking off her hat. 'What?'

'He wouldn't tell us,' said Will. 'He's been there long enough to come and speak to us if he wanted to. And he spoke to Fred, didn't he? Strikes me he wants to find something out but won't be up front about it.'

'Then why is he letting us know he's watching?' said Dorinda. She slammed her hat down on the desk. 'I *will* ask him. I'll go now.'

She marched out through the doors and up the slope to Victoria Place, her anger adding momentum to the climb. Until she was half way up and realised with a shock that her quarry had vanished.

Deflated, she plodded to the top of the slope and peered in vain for a tall figure in a brown suit. Sighing and ignoring the curious glances of the holidaymakers, she turned and went slowly back to Will and Maude.

'Gone, was he?' said Will, nodding wisely. 'Took off the minute he saw you come out, I reckon. Said he wouldn't tell us.'

There were no further sightings of the man in the brown suit during the afternoon, although as Dorinda said to Maude in the interval, he could have been prowling round the outside of the pavilion all the time they were performing. The rain that started late in the afternoon meant they had a full house for the late show, and Dorinda ended the evening in a glow of happiness and achievement.

As she approached the office, however, she was surprised to see a rather timid looking lady hovering in the foyer.

'Oh, miss! Are you the one in charge?' The lady, clutching a large brown bag in front of her like a shield, came to a quivering halt in front of her.

'Yes, I'm Dolly Alexander.' Dorinda held out her hand. A limp paw was placed into it and withdrawn quickly.

'I'm sorry – I didn't want to do this, but my husband …' she trailed off.

'Would you like to come into the office?' asked Dorinda, resigned now to deal with some kind of complaint.

'Yes, yes. Thank you.' The lady followed her into the office.

'Do sit down,' said Dorinda.

The lady still hovered.

'You see,' she said eventually, and sat down suddenly. 'I've been robbed.'

'Robbed?' Dorinda stared. 'Here, do you mean? Were you in the audience?'

'Oh, no, miss. I wouldn't – I mean, we wouldn't – no, it was this afternoon. Early.' She nodded. 'We saw your – er – people.'

'Oh, yes, handing out leaflets weren't we?'

'I didn't see you, just some others. And we got into a bit of a – well – a crowd. You know - pushed and pulled. And afterwards we found they'd gone.'

'Gone? What had?'

'Mother's pearls!'

Chapter Five

'What exactly are you saying?' asked Dorinda, forcing herself to keep calm.

'We think – that is, my husband thinks – it was one of your – er – girls.'

'And what makes him think that?' asked Dorinda. 'And, may I ask, where is he? If it was his idea to come here.'

The lady's pale pink complexion deepened. 'He had another ... he had to ...'

'I see,' said Dorinda briskly. 'And why does he think one of my young ladies should have stolen your pearls?'

'He – I – I ...' For a moment, the woman looked terrified.

'Come,' said Dorinda. 'Let's go and see the young ladies, and you can point out which one you think –'

She got no further. The woman leapt out of her chair and ran from the office. 'After her!' yelled Dorinda to Ted, who had just appeared from the auditorium. He plunged out of the door and disappeared, only to return within seconds.

'Cab,' he said succinctly. 'What happened?'

'Come backstage,' said Dorinda. She took the key from her office drawer and locked the front door. 'Just in case.'

She called the company together onstage and told them what had happened.

'Bleedin' cheek!' said Aramantha.

'But why should she do that?' asked Algy.

'She was put up to it,' said Dorinda grimly.

'Unfortunately, whoever was behind it chose badly. The woman could no more carry on that pretence than get up here and sing.'

'It's awful,' said Velda, sounding almost tearful. 'It was to blacken your name, wasn't it?'

'Mine, or The Alexandria.'

'Or the Serenaders,' put in Will.

'But vicious,' said Maude. So do we reckon it's brown suit?'

'He's a bit too obvious, isn't he?' said Will. 'I mean, he's taken the trouble to make sure we see him. '

'So that we know he's watching us,' said Dorinda. 'I think it's him.'

'And he searched the office as well?' said Velda. 'What does he look like?'

Will and Maude, having both spoken to the man, described him.

'I thought he looked lovely,' said Betty. Patsy gave her a nudge.

'I'm going to tell Fred Fowler,' said Will. 'The police ought to know someone's got it in for us.'

'And we don't want that woman complaining to the police,' said Dorinda. 'Now come on, everyone, get off back to your lodgings – and don't talk to anyone on the way home.'

She went back to the office to change into her street clothes. When she emerged, not only Will and Maude were waiting for her, but Velda Turner hovered nervously by the front door.

'Velda? Where's Maisie?'

'She's gone on ahead with Betty and Patsy.' Velda stepped forward. 'Do you really think someone's trying to harm The Alexandria? Or you?'

'It looks like it, doesn't it? The break in could have been just mischief, but the stolen pearls was so obviously more than that.'

33

Velda looked distressed. 'It's just so awful. When you've worked so hard.'

Dorinda looked at Will and Maude and raised her eyebrows. 'Don't worry about it, Velda. We'll get to the bottom of it. If we tell Constable Fowler he might be able to ...' she shrugged. 'Well, to get to the bottom of it.'

'And what was that all about?' Dorinda locked the door of The Alexandria and turned to watch Velda hurry up the slope to Victoria Place.

'She's worried,' said Maude. 'She's only just got this job. She doesn't want us closing down straight away!'

'Aramantha and Phoebe only started this season, too. They don't seem so bothered,' said Will.

'But Aramantha did calm down after I had a word with her yesterday, didn't she?' Dorinda followed her friends up to Victoria Place. 'I think she might be a bit afraid.'

'But Velda seemed really upset,' said Maude. 'She's a funny one.'

Will called on Constable Fowler the following morning. Monday wasn't a busy morning in the town – the weekend trippers were gone, the holiday makers were settled into their digs and the petty criminals were hoping for bad weather.

'Why's that, Fred?' asked Will, when Constable Fowler informed him of this.

'Folk all crowd inside, don't they? Inside your pavilion, under the pier – except we ain't got no pier – inside the pubs. Easier for a dip in amongst the crowds, ain't it?'

Dorinda laughed when Will reported this to her and Maude.

'I suppose we hope for bad weather, too, in a way. More people want to come inside to see us.'

'But too much bad weather and they'll go home again,' said Maude. 'Back to Stepney and Stockwell.'

'And Barnet and Barking,' Dorinda added. 'We ought to write a song about that.'

'Don't know about songs,' said Will, 'but Fred says he'll come along and see us in an hour, so we'd better get down to the pavilion.'

There was no sign of bad weather today, and Dorinda looked enviously down to where the new bathing tents were lined up against the cliff waiting for the more energetic holiday makers to arrive and change into their bathing suits for a refreshing swim. Nethergate had recently allowed mixed bathing, an innovation and a source of great enjoyment for the younger visitors. Dorinda hadn't tried it yet, but she was determined to get into the sea sometime before the season finished.

The Alexandria was quiet, no signs of intrusion were visible, and Dorinda settled into her office with a sigh of relief. And then she heard the scream.

Maude poked her head round the office door.

'Did you hear that?'

'Yes – I wonder what it was?'

'Some silly woman frightened in the sea, I should think,' said Maude.

But the screaming went on. Maude and Dorinda joined Will at the front door just as they saw Fred Fowler hurtling down the slope towards them.

'Fred?' called Will, but Constable Fowler ignored him and carried on round to the back of the building.

Dorinda's heart lurched, and she turned to Maude in fear. Maude pulled her back inside The Alexandria while Will followed Fowler.

After a moment the screaming stopped, and the women could hear nothing. Eventually Will appeared round the corner of the building. He shook his head, apparently unable to speak. Maude took one arm and Dorinda the other, drawing him into the foyer.

'What is it, Will?' Dorinda managed to ask, though her tongue felt as if it was sticking to the roof of her mouth.

'Dead,' muttered Will. 'She's dead.'

'Who's dead?' Maude's voice was shrill with fear.

'Velda. Velda's dead.'

'*Velda*?' Dorinda and Maude repeated together.

Will nodded. Dorinda straightened up and made for the door.

'Dolly! Wait!' Maude hurried after her. 'You can't go out there.'

Dorinda turned a white and stricken face to her friend. 'I've got to. I employed her. This could be my fault.'

'How could it be? Look, wait until Fred comes. It must be nasty, or that woman wouldn't have been screaming, and Will –' she looked back at the slumped figure of her husband, 'well, I've never seen him like this.'

Dorinda set her mouth in a grim line and shook her head, pulling away from Maude and starting towards the back of the building. Before she'd gone very far, Fred Fowler appeared, his face drained of colour.

'Miss – Dolly.' He cleared his throat. 'I was just – um – Will said ...' He came to a stop.

'You haven't left her there on her own, have you?' Dorinda's tone was sharp.

'Doctor's there.' Fowler cleared his throat again. 'He was on the prom and heard the screaming.'

'It's one of my girls, isn't it?'

'So Will said.'

Dorinda pulled herself as upright as she could. 'Do you want me to come and see?'

Fowler looked shocked. 'Oh, no Miss! I just need to ask you a few questions. I've sent for the inspector, but he can't get here from Deal that quick, see.'

Will appeared behind Dorinda and put a hand on her shoulder. 'I'll talk to Fred, Dolly. You go back to Maude.'

Maude and Dorinda sat in the foyer without speaking. Eventually, Dorinda said: 'We'll have to cancel.'

'Both performances?'

'Yes.' Dorinda stood up. 'We've got some stickers

somewhere from last year.'

Maude nodded, and they went to search the office.

Will joined them just as Dorinda found the "cancelled" stickers.

'I'll do that.' He took the stickers from her. 'Where's the paste?'

'What did Fred say?' asked Maude.

'When did we last see her, had she any enemies, what did we know about her background – you know.' He shook his head. 'I had to say we didn't know anything.'

While Will went to stick up all the "cancelled" notices, Maude went to make tea and Dorinda waited in the foyer for the arrival of the rest of her company. They all came in, bewildered and slightly scared, having seen Will and the crowd at the back of the theatre. Dorinda tried to explain.

''Ow was she killed?' Aramantha's strident voice rang out.

Surprised, Dorinda shook her head. 'I don't know. Will didn't say.'

'Didn't you go and look?' Aramantha demanded.

'Of course not! Maude and I were kept well away.'

'I want to see 'er.'

'Why?' Dorinda's surprise was reflected in the expressions of the others.

'I'm goin' to see.' Aramantha turned on a determined heel and found her way blocked by a large, red-faced man in a bowler.

'No, miss, I'd rather you didn't.' A ham-like hand ushered her backwards into the foyer. 'Miss Alexander?'

Dorinda lifted a hand. 'I'm here.' The artistes parted before her, and the red faced man beamed genially though Dorinda decided his eyes were too shrewd.

'Now, that's the way. Inspector Malkin at your service. Perhaps you'll introduce all these people?'

Dorinda crisply named each of her company.

'Very good, ma'am – I mean miss. Is this everyone?'

'There's Will, who's out pasting "cancelled" stickers on the posters, and Maude, his wife. She's making tea.'

'Tea? Now is she? That's nice. Shall we go and find her?'

Dorinda led the way, a funereal Pied Piper. Maude looked horrified.

'Now then, you're Maude …?'

'Beddowes. And I'm her husband, Will.' Will pushed through and confronted the Inspector.

'Inspector Malkin.' The shrewd eyes peered at Will. 'You found the body?'

'No!' said Will, shocked. 'Fred Fowler was already there when I arrived.'

'Ah. Haven't had much of a chance to talk to him, yet.'

'Why are you here, then?' Dorinda's voice was sharp.

'Oh, the message was "deceased part of a concert party". And she was, wasn't she?'

'She was.'

'So when did you all last see her?'

'We've already told Constable Fowler,' said Dorinda. 'He interviewed us after he'd sent for you.'

The Inspector's face lost some of its amiability.

'Don't any of you go anywhere,' he snapped. 'I shall go and consult with my – constable.'

He turned and made his way – waddled, Dorinda thought – out of the pavilion and a sigh of relief went up from the company.

'I'd better go and lock the door,' said Dorinda. 'If he wants to come back, he can knock. But we don't want the public coming in.'

'We'll still get people coming down,' said Will. 'I didn't get far with the stickers.'

'They'll see when they get to Victoria Place, though' said Dorinda. 'Maude's made tea. Just sit down and try and – um – be calm.'

She made her way through to the foyer and collected

the key from the office. As she approached the front door, it opened.

'Good morning, Miss Alexander,' said the man in the brown suit. 'My name's Jack Colyer.'

Chapter Six

Dorinda just stood and gaped. Jack Colyer's mouth lifted in a wry smile.

'Not pleased to see me, I gather.'

'I – er –' Dorinda cleared her throat. 'I'm surprised, sir.'

'Yes, you would be. Perhaps if I could come in -?'

'I'd rather you didn't.' Dorinda tried to close the door on her tormentor.

He sighed. 'I apologise if my presence near The Alexandria recently has disturbed you.'

Dorinda blinked. 'Disturbed … ?'

'I could not very well announce the fact that I was looking for Miss Velda Turner.'

Reluctantly, Dorinda opened the door. 'Why couldn't you? She was here. You could have spoken to her.'

Jack Colyer stepped inside and smiled down at her. 'But then she would have known about it, wouldn't she?'

'But why –?' Dorinda shook her head. 'Perhaps you'd better come into my office and explain.'

She led the way into the office, took her seat behind the desk and waved her unwelcome visitor to the other chair.

'Miss Turner only joined you recently, I gather?'

'Yes. But why are you interested in her? She's –'

'Dead, I know. But we wanted to know why she had come down here. Now we want to know even more.'

'Why? Who's "we"?'

'Oh, didn't I say?' He pulled a card from his pocket. 'Scotland Yard, Miss Alexander. Inspector Colyer.'

Dorinda was speechless.

'And before you ask, I have introduced myself to Inspector Malkin, whom I suspect is not exactly thrilled to see me either.'

Dorinda stood up. 'I need a cup of tea,' she said. 'May I fetch you one?'

'Thank you.' Jack Colyer inclined his head with another wry smile which clearly told her he knew how unwelcome his presence was.

Maude was coming through to the foyer. In a whisper Dorinda asked her if she could bring two cups of tea.

'He's a Scotland Yard inspector,' she explained. 'He was looking for Velda.'

Maude looked as if she might start asking questions, so Dorinda shooed her back to fetch the tea. 'Go on, I'll tell you later.'

'Now,' she said, reseating herself behind the desk. 'Perhaps you'll explain from the beginning.'

Colyer leant back in the chair, crossed his legs and steepled his fingers, staring with dark brown eyes over the top of them at Dorinda. They made her feel quite peculiar.

'Miss Velda Turner is – ah – shall we say – known to us.'

'Us?'

'The police, Miss Alexander.

'Oh. Why?'

'Let's just say she has come to our attention in the past.

'But she seemed so respectable. Not like a chorus girl at all, really.'

'You aren't much like the usual concert party manager yourself, if you don't mind me saying so.'

Dorinda felt hot colour rising up her neck just as Maude pushed open the door bearing a tray.

'Here you are, Doll – Dorinda.' She put the tray on the desk, casting a doubtful glance at Colyer.

'Thank you, Maude. I'll be out in a minute.'

'Doll?' Colyer quirked an eyebrow.

'My friends occasionally call me Dolly, not that it's any of your business.' Dorinda handed him a cup. 'Please go on with your story.'

'Not a story, exactly. Miss Turner suddenly left her London lodgings and travelled here. We wanted to know why.'

'She wanted to work here,' said Dorinda, remembering her own doubts when Velda had first arrived.

'But why? Why here? As far as we were aware she hadn't been looking for employment.'

'But why should you be aware of that? She could have been going to all the concert parties and music halls for months.'

'But she hadn't.' Colyer sipped his tea.

Dorinda regarded him thoughtfully in silence.

'We do know that,' said Colyer eventually.

'You were watching her,' said Dorinda.

'Keeping an eye on her,' amended Colyer.

'Why?'

'That doesn't matter. What does is that she came here – came *straight* here – and obtained work. Rather at the last minute, wouldn't you say? Your company had surely been formed by then.'

'It had. But she was impressive. She could sing, ballads, comedy songs – she had ideas ...' Dorinda stopped. 'What was she really?'

'A performer, very definitely,' said Colyer with a grin. 'Oh, very definitely.'

'She was not what she seemed, then,' said Dorinda.

'Rarely.'

'Was her name Velda Turner?'

'Sometimes.'

Dorinda drew an impatient breath. 'Really, Mr Colyer, or should I say Inspector, either tell me about the woman and why you are here or leave me alone to work out how to rescue my programme before I re-open.'

Jack Colyer heaved a theatrical sigh and Dorinda found her mouth twitching with amusement.

'As I said, Miss Turner was – known to us. I'm afraid I can't tell you why, but she had figured in other enquiries my colleagues had made. She had been living quietly in her lodgings, not working apparently, although able to pay her rent and buy food.'

Dorinda's eyebrows rose. 'You knew that?'

'Oh, yes, Miss Alexander. And in Clapham. Not the cheapest lodgings. And quite suddenly she left. And came here.'

Dorinda stared at her desk, tapping her fingers on her blotter. At last she looked up.

'How did you trace her, Inspector Colyer?'

He frowned at her. 'That doesn't concern you, Miss Alexander.'

'No? I think it does. The poor girl has been murdered. Outside my theatre.'

'All I need from you is anything she might have told you about her previous life. References, for instance.'

'I didn't ask for any,' said Dorinda, squashing an uncomfortable upsurge of guilt. 'She auditioned.'

'Auditioned?' Now Colyer's eyebrows rose. 'I understood you held no auditions.'

'Did you, now.' Dorinda, despite the appalling circumstances, was beginning to enjoy herself. 'I wonder who misinformed you? I auditioned in London.'

Colyer gave an involuntary gasp. '*London*?'

'Aramantha Giles and Phoebe Manners will be able to confirm that, if you care to ask them.'

Colyer's face had fallen. It was a good face, thought Dorinda, with its slightly aquiline nose, and sharp chin and those brown eyes under straight brows.

'Very well, thank you, Miss Alexander.' He stood up, placing his cup on the desk. 'If I could trouble you for the address of her lodgings here in Nethergate … ?'

Dorinda looked up at him and smiled. 'Sit down, Inspector Colyer. I didn't say I auditioned Miss Turner in London, did I?'

He looked at her for a long moment, then sat down. 'What exactly did you mean, then, Miss Alexander?'

'I auditioned Miss Giles and Miss Manners in London. I auditioned Miss Turner here, in this office.'

The straight brows shot up again. 'Then how did she …?'

'Know about us? I don't know. She said she'd heard I was hiring. She could have done, of course.'

'And do you know anything else about her?'

'She told the other girls she'd worked at The Britannia before the fire.'

'Did she?' Colyer looked thoughtful.

'Well – did she?' asked Dorinda.

'She might have done.'

'She was good enough. But The Britannia only had the greats. She might have been in the chorus – or the ballet.'

'She might.' Colyer was tapping his knee with one long finger. 'But was she?'

Dorinda sighed. 'Please, Inspector Colyer. Stop fencing with me. You were watching Velda Turner, whoever she may have been. There was a reason you were watching her and now she's dead. Does your reason have something to do with her death?'

He frowned. 'I don't know, Miss Alexander.'

Dorinda closed her eyes briefly and counted to ten. 'Then tell me why you were interested in her in the first place. Was she a supporter of Mrs Pankhurst, perhaps?'

His eyes flew to hers. 'Why would you think that?'

'Because of the way she and her supporters have been – er – treated. By the police.'

Colyer looked thoughtful. 'A supporter yourself, are you, Miss Alexander?'

'Not actively, no. But I am certainly not of the opinion

44

that men are the only people with wit enough to vote. After all, look at the woman through history who have held positions of power. At the old Queen, for instance.'

He nodded. 'Indeed. Look at yourself. To satisfy your curiosity – partially, I'm sure – Miss Turner was not being watched because of her support of the suffrage movement. As I do not know why she was here – that was why we were watching her here, to find that out – we have no idea if her death has to do with her – er – previous life.'

'Of which I'm still to be told nothing.' Dorinda was watching him closely. He smiled and stood.

'I apologise for that. I shall go and inform Inspector Malkin of our discussion and perhaps he won't come back to talk to you.'

'He will,' said Dorinda. 'He will want to speak to the girl she lodged with, won't he? And look at our dressing room.'

'Ah! You mean I should have done the same? Of course, I will, if you would prefer it, but I thought perhaps your estimable constable would be doing that?'

'Will he?' Dorinda was doubtful. 'Would that be usual?'

'I expect it would be.' Colyer held out a hand. Dorinda stood and took it. 'I shall no doubt see you again, Miss Alexander.'

'I'm sure you will.' Dorinda watched him leave the room and put her head in her hands. Murder. Now, how was The Alexandria to survive this?

Will and Maude found her in the same position five minutes later.

'Fred Fowler's been sent to look through the dressing room and talk to the others, especially Maisie,' said Will.

'Yes, he said that would happen,' said Dorinda.

'Who? That man?' asked Maude.

'Yes. Inspector Jack Colyer from Scotland Yard.'

'What did he want?'

Dorinda repeated everything Inspector Colyer had told her.

'So we're none the wiser,' said Maude.

The three of them went back to the dressing room area, where Fred Fowler, looking acutely uncomfortable, was holding court among the company.

''Ere, Miss Dolly, 'e's accusin' us of doin' away with Velda.' Predictably, Aramantha's voice was raised in protest. Fowler cast an anguished glance over his shoulder.

'No, he isn't, Aramantha,' said Dorinda calmly. 'But Velda has been – done away with. The police have to find out everything they can about her.'

'Why?' asked Phoebe. 'She's dead. They should be looking for her killer.'

Fowler opened his mouth to speak, but Dorinda held up a hand.

'But we don't know why she died. We have to know if there was any reason for someone to wish her harm, don't you see?'

'One o' these robbers, I reckon. Was she –' even the redoubtable Aramantha had to stop at the next phrase.

'She wasn't hurt that way, miss,' said Fowler, correctly interpreting the question. 'And she had a basket with her. With money in a purse.'

'So it wasn't robbery,' said Will. 'Come on, ladies. Let the constable ask his questions.'

'So, Miss – Birchall, was it? Miss Turner was lodging with you?'

'Well, sharing my room, like. At Ma Butcher's. I was there last season.'

'And did Miss Turner tell you anything about her life? Why she'd come to Nethergate?'

'No, she never. I asked her, natural like, when you've just met someone, but she never said.'

Fowler turned to the other girls. 'And did she talk to any of you?'

46

'Too 'igh and mighty,' said Aramantha. 'Thought she was better 'n the rest of us.'

'She *had* worked at The Britannia,' put in Patsy timidly.

'Where's that?' asked Fowler. Nine pairs of eyes turned on him with incredulity. He eased his collar. 'Classy, then?'

'I'll tell you all about it one day, Fred,' said Will. 'But she told us she'd worked there. We don't know if she actually had. Dolly – Miss Alexander didn't ask for references.'

'No, Miss?' Fowler's eyebrows rose.

'No.' Dorinda felt her colour rising again, to her annoyance. 'I know I should have. I'm very lax about that sort of thing, I prefer to trust my instincts.'

'You didn't ask for my references either, Miss,' said Phoebe. Aramantha kept quiet.

'Then Miss Turner could have come from anywhere?' said Fowler. 'And could have been anybody? Not Velda Turner at all?'

Chapter Seven

Fred Fowler sighed and turned to Algy and Ted.

'You two gentlemen. Miss Turner didn't confide in you?'

Algy shook his head.

'Not her,' said Ted. 'She was good on stage, mind, but sort of closed down as soon as she came off.'

There were murmurs of agreement from the rest of the company.

'We'll, have to go and have a look at this room at Ma – Mrs Butcher's, I suppose.' Fowler turned to Dorinda. 'Can I take Miss – Maisie away?'

'Yes, of course, Constable,' said Dorinda, taking his arm and drawing him away from the others. 'But I just wanted to tell you that there's a Scotland Yard man here. He's been questioning me about Miss Turner.'

'He has?' Fowler looked astonished. 'Why wasn't I told?'

'I don't think Inspector Malkin had time to tell you. And you know him already.'

'I do?'

'The gentleman you met behind the pavilion the other day. Remember.'

'Him? He's a policeman?'

'An Inspector from Scotland Yard, yes. From that new Detective branch, I expect. Although it isn't that new any more, is it?'

'Well.' Fowler brooded for a moment. 'I'd better go and see the Inspector – Malkin, that is – about what I do next.'

'You won't be wanting Maisie now, then?'

'Not right now, Miss, thank you.' He shook his head. 'What a mess, eh?'

Dorinda walked back to company, deep in thought.

'What do we do now, Dolly?' asked Ted. 'We're not going on today, are we?'

'No, we can't. You can all go home, but if you could be here early tomorrow I'd be grateful.'

'Why?' asked – inevitably – Aramantha.

'Because we'll have to go through new material,' said Algy.

'New? Why?'

'Not necessarily new, dear, just revised. We'll have to set things differently, won't we?' said Maude.

'I can do all 'er stuff,' said Aramantha.

'But then you'd be missing in other places, wouldn't you?' said Dorinda. 'I'll work out the new settings today and we'll go through them in the morning.'

In ones and twos they drifted out until only Will, Maude and Dorinda were left.

'Will I pop out to the pie shop?' asked Maude. 'We could all do with something to eat.'

'Oh, yes, Maude, thank you.' Dorinda went to find her purse.

'I'll check out what's happening at the back,' said Will.

Alone, Dorinda went to the piano and began leafing through her sheet music. Thankfully, she hadn't altered many of the numbers when Velda joined the company, other than to give her two solos and change some of the sketches. She took the music into the office, found paper and pencil and began to change everything back.

Maude appeared ten minutes later with the hot pies.

'Will not back?'

Dorinda shook her head. 'I wouldn't have thought he'd want to hang around there, though.'

'There's not much of a crowd there now,' said Maude.

'I reckon they must have taken her away.'

'Wouldn't we have heard?'

'Don't know. Here – have your pie.'

Either side of the desk, the two women were half way through their delectable picnic when the door opened and Will came in looking worried.

'I'm sorry, Dolly – I couldn't help it!'

'Help what?' asked Dorinda, startled, and then saw what. Will was followed in by Inspector Malkin and Inspector Colyer, both looking grim.

'Gentlemen.' Dorinda stood, surreptitiously trying to brush crumbs from her fingers and, deplorably, from her skirt.

'Please sit down, Miss,' said Malkin. 'And you too, ma'am,' as Maude rose to leave.

'What's this about?' asked Dorinda, sitting down and gripping her greasy fingers together to stop them shaking.

'Well, miss, see – we've found out about your past.' Malkin leered across the desk.

'My – past? What on earth are you talking about? I was a governess before I joined the Wanderers. I haven't got a past.'

Will was making faces at her over Malkin's shoulder, and her stomach swooped. Controlling her features, she swallowed and tried to look politely interested.

'Ah, but there was the case of a certain stolen necklace, wasn't there?' Malkin's small, sharp eyes were boring into hers. She swallowed again.

'Inspector.' Jack Colyer's smooth voice broke in. 'I can't think that has any relevance here.'

'I'll say what has relevance and what doesn't.' Malkin was clearly unhappy with the intervention of the Scotland Yard man. 'This is Nethergate business.'

'Yes, and it was cleared up quite satisfactorily, I believe.' Colyer was studying his fingernails.

Malkin's face was turning purple. 'This woman was

accused of stealing a diamond necklace!'

Maude opened her mouth but at a signal from Colyer, she shut it again.

'And wasn't it discovered to have been a mistake?' he asked.

'In public!' Maude burst out in spite of herself.

Malkin turned on her. 'You be quiet!'

'Inspector.' Colyer's voice was now as smooth as ice. 'I believe Constable Fowler told us what had happened as far as he knew, and I'm perfectly sure it will have been recorded somewhere at your station. Meanwhile, we were going to ask Miss Alexander and Mr and Mrs Beddowes what their recollections of the event were, as I recall.'

Malkin made a sound like a boiling kettle and glared at Colyer.

'I'll ask, shall I?' said Colyer, with a smile.

Dorinda felt the tension drain away, and looking at Will and Maude saw them relax. Will came and stood behind Maude's chair and Colyer came and perched on the edge of Dorinda's desk.

'Now,' he said. 'About this necklace.'

Will, Maude and Dorinda looked at each other. Eventually, Dorinda took a deep breath.

'The necklace belonged to my employer, Mrs Shepherd. Just after I – left, it was discovered to be missing.'

'You didn't leave *because* the necklace was missing?'

'No, she certainly didn't,' said Will forcefully.

'It's all right, Will,' said Dorinda. 'No, I left because I joined Will's Wanderers as a pianist.'

Colyer's straight brows rose in surprise. 'You left a good job as a governess to join a Pierrot troupe?'

Dorinda saw Will grip Maude's shoulder. 'Yes,' she said. 'Maude made me a costume overnight and I went to stay with them. And then I was accused of stealing the necklace. Right here on the sands.'

'Someone fetched a constable – not Fred Fowler, an old boy called – Barrett, was it, Maude? – and he was here when someone came down from the house and said it had been found. Showed it to everyone, too.' Will nodded, satisfied with his statement.

'It was reported in the paper,' said Maude, nervously. 'Wasn't it, Dolly?'

Dorinda nodded, deciding it was safer to keep quiet now.

'Where was it found?' asked Colyer, his eyes not moving from Dorinda's face.

'In the house, of course,' said Will, surprised.

'By whom?'

'Sir Frederick Anderson,' said Dorinda. 'Mrs Shepherd's father.'

'Oh? How was that?'

'It had been a gift from him to his late wife, Mrs Shepherd's mother. It turned out that Mrs Shepherd never liked it, so Sir Frederick had taken it back.'

'And had no one asked Mrs Shepherd?'

Will, Maude and Dorinda had no answer to this.

'So there is a bit of a mystery about this necklace.' Colyer smiled. 'But quite clearly it isn't anything to do with Miss Alexander.' He turned to Malkin who was muttering to himself in the corner. 'Shall we go and have a look at your station records, Inspector? I expect we can find out a little more there.' He nodded to Dorinda, Maude and Will. 'Ladies and gentleman.'

Silence followed the two officers' departure. Eventually, Dorinda stood up, went to the front door and locked it.

'What do we do now?' asked Maude.

'There's nothing we can do,' said Dorinda, trying to quell a feeling of panic. 'I don't remember the whole story being reported in the newspapers, but if they care to, I'm sure the police could find it out. They won't find all of the truth, however.'

'It can't have anything to do with Velda's death,' said Will. 'Can it?'

'How?' asked Dorinda. 'I was accused of stealing a necklace. I was proved innocent before I was anywhere near a police station. How could the –' she hesitated, 'the murder of a London chorus girl have anything to do with that?'

'The Shepherds came from London,' said Maude.

'You lived there with them yourself before you came here,' said Will.

'But neither they nor I live there now,' said Dorinda. She took a turn about the room. 'I think I shall go and visit them. I ought to tell Sir Frederick about the – er – about Velda. After all, he is part owner of The Alexandria.'

'He told you to consider yourself the sole owner,' said Will. 'I was there, remember.'

'He still ought to know. Especially now that Inspector has dragged in the necklace.' Dorinda sat down at her desk. 'I shall write a note to Ivy.'

Maude looked dubious. 'Will you wait for a reply? If you do, by the time she sends it, we'll be open again, and you'll never get over to Anderson Place and back again for the first performance.'

Dorinda looked up. 'You're right. Do you think I should go today?'

'Yes.' Will slapped his thighs. 'And we'll go with you. Oh – we wouldn't presume to visit Sir Frederick, but May and Ellen are still with them. We could see them. Best you don't go on your own.'

'I'd like that,' said Dorinda with relief. 'I was wondering how I would get there, but we can hire a cab, perhaps?'

'Better than that,' said Will with a grin. 'I always borrow old Blower's trap when we go and visit Maude's ma. He'll let us take that.'

'Will he? Who's Blower?'

'Sells veg. But he's lazy. He goes out in the mornings for a spell, comes back in time for his missis's stew and goes to sleep for the afternoon. Come on, let's lock up here and go and see him. You all right, Maude?'

'Yes.' Maude stood up. 'I'd like to see May and Ellen – and Ivy, if we can. And Anderson Place. It sounds beautiful.'

As they walked up the slope to Victoria Place, Constable Fowler appeared at the top.

'I'm not supposed to let you leave, Will.' He looked uncomfortable.

'What?' Dorinda gasped. 'On whose orders? And why?'

'Inspector Malkin, Miss. And he didn't say why.'

'Don't be silly, Fred Fowler,' said Maude. 'He can't keep us locked up in there with no reason. And don't you try and arrest us. We'll be back at our lodgings later. You can find us there.'

She pushed past him followed meekly by Will and Dorinda, leaving Fowler scratching his head under his helmet.

Old Blower, who lived at the top of the town in a ramshackle cottage, proved only too willing to lend his trap and fat piebald pony, Brutus.

'Loves that 'orse better'n me,' chuckled Old Blower's wife, pocketing the coins Dorinda had given her. 'All right getting him hitched up?'

Will was already on his way to fetch Brutus from his scrubby little field where he nodded sleepily by the fence. Maude, obviously used to the procedure, was opening the door to the shed where the trap was kept. It had once been painted blue and red, but most of the paint had rubbed off and it had a rather sad air about it.

Brutus backed slowly and resignedly into position. Dorinda patted him on the nose. 'Sorry to drag you out,' she whispered. As they left the yard, he turned automatically to go down to the town, and proved slightly recalcitrant when Will turned him firmly towards the open country, especially when he realised he was going to have to climb a hill. However, he broke into a trot, ears pricked forward, when Nethergate dropped behind them, and the road led between farmland. Away to their left lay the villages of Heronsbourne, Cherry Ashton and Steeple Mount and at last they drove down Steeple Martin's main street and out the other side. After another three miles, the imposing gateposts of Anderson Place appeared.

'We're here,' said Dorinda.

Chapter Eight

'I can't leave the trap here,' Will whispered as he drew to a halt just inside the gates. 'Can I get round the back?'

Dorinda pointed. 'Through there. It leads to the stables.'

Brutus obediently plodded round the side of the house. Will had barely reined him to a halt when a door opened and three people tumbled through it.

'Dorinda! Will! Maude!' shouted the first woman, a tall blonde figure wearing an elegant purple dress.

The other two women, one short and slim, the other plump and beaming, wore traditional servants' dress.

Amid a flurry of greetings, Will managed to ask if there was somewhere he could leave Brutus and the trap. A smiling lad appeared and led the pony away, and the three visitors were ushered into the kitchen.

'How lovely!' said Dorinda looking round. 'Are you pleased with your new kitchen, May?'

The plump cook nodded enthusiastically. 'Oh, yes, Miss! Course you seen it afore Sir Fred 'ad it done up modern, didn't you?'

'Oh, don't call me Miss! Dorinda – or Dolly, if you like. And Ivy – I'm sure you had a hand in the kitchen, didn't you?'

Elegant Ivy winked. 'Course I did! Freddie wouldn't know where to start.'

'Ellen – how's Miss Julia?'

'She's well, Miss – Dolly. She'll want to see you.' The little maid bobbed her head.

'Come on, then,' said Ivy. 'What's brought the three of

you out here? You've started the season, haven't you? Not playing today?' She looked from one to the other of her three guests. 'You can tell me all about it. Shall we have a cuppa, May?'

'Kettle's already on,' said May. 'We stayin' down 'ere? Aren't you goin' to take Miss – Dolly up to see Sir Fred?'

'Not just yet. We'll have a cuppa here, eh?' Ivy sat down with an expensive rustle. The others gathered round the huge scrubbed table and looked expectantly at Dorinda.

'It's not pleasant,' she said. 'It's – oh, I don't know where to begin.'

'We had a new chorus girl start just before the start of the season,' Will took over. 'She kept herself to herself, but she was good. Very talented. And then, this morning, she got herself murdered.'

The three Anderson Place residents gasped, and Ellen shrieked.

'Murder!'

'And the police are looking into it,' said Dorinda.

'And this Inspector found out about the necklace,' blurted Maude.

Ivy looked surprised. 'What of it?'

'This Malkin seemed to think Dolly was a criminal,' said Will. 'Although the other Inspector didn't.'

'Stop there, Will,' said Ivy, as May shook her head and stood up to make the tea. 'You've lost us. Dolly, from the beginning.'

So, while May set the big brown teapot on the table with the thick kitchen cups, Dorinda told the whole story, including the wrecked office and the false theft report.

'And the Scotland Yard inspector knows something about Velda Turner, and I think he's sure that it's the reason for her murder,' Dorinda concluded. 'But the inspector from Deal doesn't.'

'Sounds to me as if the Deal inspector don't like

Scotland Yard butting in,' said Ivy.

'I know,' said Dorinda, 'but they were both going back to the police station to look up the records.'

'Well, they won't find much, will they?' said Ivy robustly. 'And if you like, I'll put the bloody thing on and march down there and show 'em. Like I did before, remember?'

They all smiled at the memory of Ivy throwing off her new coat in the middle of the promenade to display the dazzling Anderson diamonds.

'I know you would, Ivy.' Dorinda reached over and squeezed Ivy's hand. 'I really don't want them looking any deeper, though.'

'They've got no bloomin' reason to,' said Ellen.

They all looked at each in silence for a moment until the kitchen door was flung open and two maids in black uniforms hurried in and came to a surprised halt when they saw Ivy.

Ellen stood up. 'These two are Connie and Edie, our new maids.'

Connie and Edie bobbed uncertain curtsies and looked nervously at Ivy, who laughed.

'It's all right, girls, you ought to be used to me by now. These people are friends of ours.' She waved a hand at May and Ellen. 'This is Miss Alexander, and these two are Mr and Mrs Beddowes.'

The two maids nodded, cast a look at May and scuttled back out of the kitchen.

'They'll never get used to our ways,' sighed May.

'No more'n the local toffs will, either,' said Ivy.

'Don't they call?' asked Dorinda.

'They all did – just the once. At least we give 'em something to talk about. Funnily enough, the vicar's wife's all right.'

'She's one o' *them*, though,' said Ellen with a sniff.

'One of what?' asked Will.

'Suffrage people. You know, Pankhurst and her lot.'

'Is she?' Dorinda brightened. 'Is there a group near here?'

'Oh, Dolly, you aren't, are you?' cried May.

'Don't you believe women and men should be equal, May?' asked Dorinda.

'Don't see 'ow we can be,' said May simply. 'Made different, ain't we?'

Ivy laughed. 'I agree with Dolly, but I don't reckon there's much use in fighting about it. Anyway, I don't have to.'

'No, you always get your way without a fight,' said Ellen.

'How is Mrs Shepherd? And Julia?' asked Dorinda. 'Does she mind living here?'

'She's as happy as she can be. She says they ought to be living in the Dower House but I'm not having that,' said Ivy. 'They've got their own set of rooms, and I try and make her come and join us for meals, but she says we need our privacy.' Ivy laughed. 'Can't think why!'

'And Miss Julia's right as a bright penny,' said Ellen. 'Quite grown up, she is, now.'

'And the boys?'

'Still at school. Be home soon for the summer,' said Ivy. 'They were a bit difficult with me at first – well, you know that. At their posh school it's not done for a grandfather to marry his servant.'

'There must be a lot of grandfathers who married chorus girls, though,' said Maude.

'That's different, somehow,' said Ivy. 'Anyhow, I'm going to take Dorinda up to see Freddie and Nemone now. You be all right down here for a bit, Maude? Will?'

'Fine, thanks, Ivy,' said Maude.

'Are you really enjoying life, Ivy?' Dorinda asked, as Ivy led her through the green baize door.

'Gawd love yer, Dolly! Course I am. And I'm doing me

bit for equality, too. See those two girls, Connie and Edie? Well, they thought they'd be coming here and working their little fingers to the bone as scullery maids or some such, and Ellen, May and me starts treating them as friends. Couldn't get over it, they couldn't. Course, they still have to do the whole maid thing for Freddie and Nemone, but there's none of this turning your back when the master walks through, and there's no butler, nor no housekeeper to turn you off if you so much as drops a spoon.'

Dorinda nodded as they started up the wide staircase. 'And you actually call Mrs Shepherd Nemone, now?'

'It took a while, but she kept on at me.' Ivy turned a brilliant smile on her friend. 'After all, I owe her a lot. It was Nemone who persuaded me I should accept Sir Freddie. And him her dad, too. It's a miracle.'

'She did a lot for me, too,' said Dorinda. 'As did you and Sir Fred.'

'Bless you, no more than you deserve. Now here we are.'

Ivy knocked on a door and received an invitation to come in.

'Look who I've brought to see you, Nemone!' Ivy delivered Dorinda as though she were a particularly delightful present.

'Oh, my dear!' Nemone Shepherd rose from her chair and almost ran across the room to embrace Dorinda.

Ivy recounted Dorinda's story after one look at the other two women, who were both tearful as they remembered the past. 'If you've stopped snivelling enough to speak, did I tell it right?'

Dorinda nodded, wiping her eyes with a handkerchief provided by Mrs Shepherd.

'It sounds appalling, Dorinda. But there can be no question of the police finding anything else in your background, can there?' Mrs Shepherd, sat up straight and tucked her own handkerchief neatly into her sleeve.

'Well,' began Dorinda.

'I've told her, I'll put the bloody diamonds on and go and show 'em,' said Ivy.

'It's not that,' said Dorinda.

'I know,' said both the other women together.

'Come on, let's go and see Sir Freddie. When will Julia be back, Nemone?'

'Oh, quite soon, I think.' Mrs Shepherd looked at the ornate ormolu clock on the high mantelpiece. 'She goes to lessons with a Mrs Porter in the village, you see Dorinda. She shares them with Mrs Porter's daughter.'

'That's the vicar's wife I told you about, Dolly,' said Ivy as they left the room. 'Now, come along. We'll see Julia when she comes home. And you will stay for dinner, won't you?'

'I think that will be too late for us,' said Dorinda. 'We've got to drive back to Nethergate and get the pony and trap back to its owner.'

'We could have taken you in the motor car,' said Ivy proudly. 'Yes – my Freddie's learnt to drive. Although we've got Billy – who took care of your pony – he's odd job man and now the chauffeur as well, if we want him. Very grand we are, sweeping about the countryside.'

She stopped beside large double doors and threw them open.

'Look who's here, Freddie!'

Sir Frederick, tall, thin, with abundant white hair and moustache, rose creakily to greet her.

'My dear Dorinda! How lovely to see you! How are you, and how's The Alexandria?'

Dorinda glanced at Ivy as she took Sir Frederick's hand. 'Well, that's why I'm here, sir.'

'Don't sir me! I'm Freddie to Ivy – I should be Freddie to you too.' He patted her cheek with a long finger. 'After all, we're in business together, aren't we? Now, sit down

61

and tell me about it.'

But again, it was Ivy who told him, afraid retelling the story would upset Dorinda again.

'I don't see what you're worried about, my dear,' said Sir Frederick when she'd finished. 'You've done nothing wrong!'

'Well …' said Dorinda doubtfully.

'You haven't!' said Ivy strongly. 'No matter what stupid old biddies think.'

'Despite her use of strong language, I agree with her,' said Sir Frederick with a twinkle at his wife.

'She won't stay to dinner, Freddie,' said Ivy. 'She and Will and Maude have come in a trap from Nethergate and they've got to get back.'

'I'd like to see Will and Maude. Where have you hidden them?'

Ivy laughed. 'They're in the kitchen with May and Ellen. Shall I bring them up?'

'Do, please, my love.' As Ivy swept out of the room, Sir Frederick turned back to Dorinda. 'Now, my dear. You must not worry about this. It sounds as though this policeman is trying to make trouble. Perhaps he doesn't approve of women in business.'

'There are a lot of people like that, Sir Freddie. Although in my business perhaps it's more acceptable because the business itself is seen as not quite respectable.'

'We can't change the world in a few years, Dorinda. Maybe these women who are fighting for the vote will make a difference one day.'

'Dorinda sighed. 'I would like to think so, even though I don't agree with some of the violence they use. But I do feel that I'm the equal of a man.'

'Of course you are. So's my Ivy. You're both young, but poor Nemone, now, she was brought up to think she could do nothing for herself and must submit to the will of her parents and eventually – her husband.' Sir Frederick

62

sighed. 'And look where that got us all.' He looked at Dorinda shrewdly. 'That's what you're worrying about, isn't it?'

'Yes.' Dorinda nodded. 'I don't want to harm anybody.'

'You won't,' said Sir Frederick firmly, as the doors were flung open again and Will and Maude were ushered in. Before long they were joined by Nemone and her daughter Julia, who threw herself into her former governess's arms. Shortly after that, Ellen and May arrived with trayloads of food and it appeared Ivy had ordered what she called "a proper nursery tea" since the visitors would not stay to dinner.

'We're terribly informal here, you see, Dorinda,' said Nemone Shepherd, refilling Dorinda's cup. 'The new maids couldn't get used to it.'

'So Ivy was telling me,' said Dorinda. 'All very enlightened. Not even a footman to wait on you!'

'We only had a small staff in the London house, didn't we? And we managed. Just because we've got a bigger house now, thanks to Father, there's no reason to suppose we can't manage now.'

'And I can still work,' said Ivy. 'I'd get bored if I didn't have something to do, apart from look after my old darling here.'

Her old darling smiled fondly at her and patted her hand. 'Have you heard the new word "egalitarian", Dorinda?'

Dorinda shook her head looking puzzled, while Ivy rolled her eyes. 'Too clever by half, he is,' she said.

'It comes from the French and means –' Sir Frederick frowned. 'Equality of mankind, I think. That's what we are here at Anderson Place. We're very egalitarian.'

'And so say all of us,' said Ivy.

Chapter Nine

'Will it work, do you think?' Dorinda asked, as she, Will and Maude bowled along behind Brutus on the way back to Nethergate.

'What?'

'The Anderson Place household. They're being ostracised by all the people of their own type. What will that do to the children?'

'Young Julia seems happy enough,' said Maude. 'She was telling me all about cooking in Mrs Porter's kitchen. She said May won't let her do it at The Place.'

'But she's young. In a few years she'll want to be going out with young people of her own age. She should be presented, really.'

'Would she have been presented if they'd still been living in the London house?' said Will.

'I don't know,' said Dorinda. 'She's only the granddaughter of a baronet, not a daughter, so perhaps she wouldn't. It's not something I heard much about as a pupil teacher at the school.'

'You've never told us much about that, Dolly,' said Maude. 'What was it like? And how did you get from there to Mrs Shepherd?'

'Oh – that was easy! Mrs Shepherd had gone there herself. I was put there by my guardian when I was very young because my parents were dead, and I stayed.'

'Why didn't your guardian take you in?' asked Will.

'Oh, he was a fusty old solicitor. I only ever saw him twice. I believe there was no one else to take charge when my parents died.'

'Oh, you must have been so unhappy!' said Maude.

'I wasn't actually.' Dorinda smiled into the darkness. 'I was so young when I arrived at the school I don't really remember anything before then, and the teachers were so kind. Most of them, anyway. And the owner was wonderful. Miss Birtwhistle, her name was, naturally known by everyone as Bertie.'

'I thought those schools were a bit – hard, you know?' said Will.

'Yes, I think a lot of them were, but Bertie was very modern in her thinking. She was a great admirer of Mary Wollstonecraft.'

'Who?' said Will and Maude together.

Dorinda laughed. 'Have you heard of a book called *Frankenstein?*'

They both shook their heads.

'Well, it doesn't matter. But Mary's daughter wrote that. And Mary wrote a book called *A Vindication of the Rights of Woman*. Very popular with a certain group of women at the moment, I'm told.'

'Oh, I see. That's why …' Maude stopped.

'Why what?'

'Nothing.'

Dorinda was sure Maude was blushing in the darkness.

'Why I'm so confident I can do everything myself?' she suggested. 'Yes, I'm sure it is. But I'm not sure the county is ready for Sir Freddie's "egalitarian" experiment yet.'

'He's a lovely old boy, though, isn't he?' said Will. 'I've got a lot of time for Sir Freddie.'

'It's thanks to him we've all got jobs, so I should think you have,' said Dorinda.

'No, Dolly, it's thanks to you starting the Silver Serenaders when Will had his head turned and went off up north,' said Maude. 'If you hadn't done that, we would never have bought the pitch.'

'So I did you a favour by going up north,' said Will,

giving his wife a dig in the ribs. She slapped his hand and giggled. Dorinda looked away.

By the time they had walked back to their lodgings after delivering Brutus and his trap safely back to Old Blower, it was late. As Will let them in, their landlady appeared from her back kitchen.

'There you are!' she said, wringing her hands. 'I thought you was never coming back!'

'Why?' said Will. 'It isn't even ten yet. We're never home this early.'

'It's those police. They've been here asking for you all afternoon.'

Dorinda groaned.

'Which police?' asked Maude. 'Fred Fowler?'

'No, not him.' The landlady dismissed Fowler scornfully. 'No some big bloke with a red face and a tall one who looked like a gent.'

'Both of them!' said Will. 'Now, what did they want?'

'Did they say they would come back?' asked Dorinda.

'Just said to tell you they was looking for you. I don't know, I'm sure. I don't hold with the police coming round.'

'No,' said Dorinda wryly. 'At the moment, neither do I.'

They were not disturbed during the night, but early next morning Dorinda was woken by the landlady knocking on her door.

'Miss!' she hissed. 'They're here again.'

'Dorinda sat up sleepily. 'Who is?'

'Those police. They're downstairs. The fat one nearly come up here himself.'

Dorinda sighed. 'All right. Tell them to give me ten minutes.'

Ten minutes later a silver-costumed Pierrot entered the landlady's parlour.

'What the …!' exploded Inspector Malkin.

'You gave me no time to dress myself properly,' said Dorinda demurely. 'This was the best I could do.'

Inspector Colyer's lips were twitching.

'So, do sit down gentlemen.' Dorinda sat on an upright chair near the door. 'And please tell me what is so urgent that you were asking for us all afternoon yesterday and so early this morning.'

Inspector Malkin was spluttering again.

'I'm afraid my colleague was under the impression that you had – er – what was the word you used, Malkin?"

'Skedaddled!' roared Malkin.

'Why?' Dorinda was amused.

'There was very little in his reports about the theft of a diamond necklace or its recovery, and Inspector Malkin noticed that you had left your employment at the same time as the theft. Therefore – you had taken it.'

'I thought we went through this yesterday morning?' said Dorinda, making her voice as icy as possible.

'I apologise, Miss Alexander, but it is our duty to look into it.'

'Undoubtedly,' said Dorinda, 'but what it has to do with the murder of Velda Turner I fail to understand.'

'So do I,' muttered Colyer, before turning to Malkin. 'Well, Inspector?'

'You'll come to the police station with me now, if you don't mind,' said Malkin, moving towards Dorinda.

'Oh, I *do* mind.' Dorinda was on her feet. 'I will not accompany you anywhere. And I suggest you get in touch immediately with Sir Frederick Anderson, of Anderson Place. He and his family are aware of the present circumstances and I believe they can help you.'

Colyer shook his head with a rueful grin. 'See, Malkin? I told you. Now you'd better send Fowler off on his bicycle to this Anderson Place, hadn't you?'

'This is bluff!' Malkin was roaring again, and the landlady appeared nervously in the doorway.

'I'm sorry,' said Dorinda. 'Could you see if Mr or Mrs Beddowes is available?' The landlady vanished.

'What is the matter with him?' Dorinda asked Colyer. 'Apoplexy?'

Malkin sat down suddenly and began mopping his forehead with a large handkerchief.

'Frustration,' said Colyer mildly. 'Murder is not the sort of crime he has to deal with. Not this kind of murder. And you did rather fuel his suspicions by running off yesterday.'

'Running off?' Dorinda almost squeaked. 'The three of us went visiting since we had been forced to cancel the show.'

'May I ask where?' Colyer was very polite.

'Yes. Anderson Place.'

Both inspectors looked at her in surprise.

'*All* of you?' asked Colyer after a moment.

'Yes. All of us. We know the household.'

At that moment, Will walked into the room.

Malkin looked up listlessly. Colyer stood.

'Mr Beddowes. Sorry to disturb you, but could you tell us where you were yesterday afternoon?'

'Yes – we were at Anderson Place.' Will looked at both inspectors in bewilderment. 'Why?'

'Because Inspector Malkin couldn't find you,' said Colyer wearily and sat down again.

Will suddenly noticed Dorinda in her Silver Serenaders costume. 'Whatever are you doing, Dolly?'

'He didn't give me time to get dressed properly,' said Dorinda, by now enjoying herself.

Maude burst into the room.

'Dolly! What are they doing to you?'

'Nothing, Maude.' Dorinda stood up and patted Maude's arm. 'They want to know why we went to see the Andersons yesterday.'

'I think,' said Jack Colyer, also standing, 'in view of

68

the information we've received this morning, Inspector Malkin, we have no need to detain Miss Alexander any longer.'

'Eh?' Malkin looked up, bewildered.

'The fact that Miss Alexander and Mr and Mrs Beddowes all went to visit Sir Frederick Anderson yesterday would seem to argue that Miss Alexander did not steal any diamond necklaces from the family, would it not?'

'We don't know they went there,' mumbled Malkin, staring at his boots.

'Oh, I think they did,' said Colyer. 'Come along, man. We have work to do. Good morning, Miss Alexander, Mrs Beddowes. I'm sorry to have bothered you.'

Silence followed the policemen's departure. At last, Dorinda went to the window and peered out.

'They've gone.'

'Will they go and see Sir Fred?' asked Maude.

'Maybe. But I don't think we have anything to worry about now, do you?' said Will. 'Dolly, you've done nothing wrong, neither now nor in the past, so stop worrying about it.'

'I know,' said Dorinda with a sigh. 'I shouldn't have worried about it at all, should I? But I could hardly tell that Inspector Malkin what really happened, could I?'

'I could,' said Will.

'Will!' Maude was shocked. 'You dare!'

'I don't think it's fair,' said Will. 'Dolly shouldn't have to worry about something that was nothing to do with her.'

'That's hardly true, is it, Will?' said Dorinda wryly, 'but I agree. It isn't fair. Perhaps in a hundred years things will be different for women, but that won't help me,'

'You know what I'd like to do,' said Will, sometime later as the three of them strolled down towards The Alexandria. 'I'd like to buy a little cottage so we could stay here all year.'

69

At the end of the season they all went back to London and hoped for work in the supper rooms or at private concerts. Maude took in sewing, and Dorinda, as a pianist was probably the best placed of the three in that she was frequently booked as an accompanist.

'What would we do here in the winter?' asked Maude.

'You took in pupils, didn't you, Dolly, when you stayed that year?' said Will.

'Yes,' said Dorinda shortly, not wishing to be reminded of that particular winter.

'It would be nice, though,' said Maude wistfully. 'I always like it here before the season starts.'

Dorinda had come to a stop.

'What does he want now?' she muttered. Will and Maude followed her eyes and saw Inspector Jack Colyer leaning on the railings above The Alexandria.

'It'll be about Velda,' said Maude. 'I knew that woman was trouble the minute I saw her.'

Chapter Ten

'Of course it'll be about Velda,' said Dorinda, 'but what more can we tell him?'

'Let's go and find out,' said Will. 'Can't stand here all day long.'

Colyer turned at their approach. For once, he was wearing a hat, which he raised politely.

'Mrs Beddowes, Miss Alexander. Beddowes. I wonder if I could persuade you to walk a little with me, Miss Alexander?'

Three sets of eyebrows shot up.

'W – walk?' stammered Dorinda.

'I want to apologise for the rather heavy handed attempt to talk to you this morning.'

'Thank you, but there's no need to say more. I accept your apology,' said Dorinda, making as if to step round him.

'And to ask you a couple of questions,' said Colyer, as if she hadn't spoken.

Dorinda closed her eyes.

'Go on, Dolly,' said Will. 'Give us the key. We'll open up.'

Wordlessly, Dorinda handed over the key. Colyer tipped his hat to Maude and held out his arm to Dorinda, who eyed it warily.

'It won't bite, said Colyer, 'but naturally, if you prefer ...' He dropped his arm to his side. He turned towards the town and began to stroll along Victoria Parade. Dorinda fell into step beside him.

'What did you want to ask me?'

He turned his head and looked down at her. 'I wondered how an obviously educated young lady comes to be managing a seaside concert party.'

'And theatre,' said Dorinda, lifting her chin.

'Ah. And are you going to answer me?'

'I'm managing them because I own them,' said Dorinda, and had the gratification of seeing Jack Colyer so taken aback that he came to a sudden halt.

'You *own* them?'

Dorinda smirked.

'I – I'm sorry. I assumed ...' Colyer was floundering.

'It isn't so unusual these days, you know,' said Dorinda, turning and deliberately continuing to stroll along Victoria Place, forcing him to hurry to catch her up. 'There are many women in business – especially in our business.'

'I – yes, of course.' Colyer suddenly threw back his head and laughed. Dorinda smiled with him. 'I'm so sorry. I was guilty of making assumptions, something a policeman should never do.'

'I'm afraid women are used to that,' said Dorinda. 'Now, perhaps you'll ask me those other questions.'

By this time, they had reached the square, overlooked by the venerable Swan Hotel. Colyer continued past it.

'I'm afraid you'll find them impertinent.' He took his pipe out of his pocket and chewed the stem.

'Ask, and we'll see.'

He was silent until they had crossed the square and started down Harbour Street.

'There was something you didn't want to tell us when you were asked about the theft of the diamond necklace. I believe there was more to the story.'

Dorinda looked straight ahead.

'None of you answered when we asked why no one had asked your employer if she knew where the necklace was. That seemed odd.'

'It wasn't Mrs Shepherd who accused me of the theft.'

'No? And it wasn't Sir Frederick, because it was he who had taken it.' He paused. 'So who was it, Dorinda?'

Dorinda gasped.

'I'm sorry. It could have been more familiar – I could have called you Dolly.' His mouth lifted in a lopsided grin. 'Miss Alexander, I apologise – again. Who accused you of theft?'

Dorinda stopped and turned to lean on the railings that topped the harbour wall. 'It was Mrs Shepherd's' – she paused – 'husband.'

'Ah.' Colyer was silent for a moment. 'So he saw the necklace was missing – going through his wife's jewellery, was he? – and immediately decided you had stolen it. Now why was that?'

Dorinda sighed. 'I told you yesterday, I had just left to join Will's Wanderers.'

'And I asked why you would do such a thing.'

Dorinda fixed her eyes on the little rocky island in the middle of the bay. 'Because I was young and stupid and I fell for the youngest member of the troupe.'

Neither she nor Colyer broke the subsequent silence for some time. At last he turned back towards the town.

'May I buy you a cup of tea?'

She looked at him, surprised. 'Thank you, but no. I must get back to The Alexandria. I asked the company to be early today to rehearse the new staging.'

'New … ?'

'Because of Velda's death, we are one actress short, so I have to rearrange the songs and sketches.'

'I see, of course' He continued walking beside her in silence until they reached the slope leading down to The Alexandria.

'No more questions?' said Dorinda, turning towards him.

'Not at the moment.' He held out a hand. 'That was very brave of you.'

'Brave?' She took his hand. 'What was brave?'

'Admitting the reason you joined Will's Wanderers.'

'Oh.' Dorinda felt tell-tale colour creeping into her cheeks and pulled her hand away.

'Before you go,' said Colyer, turning slightly away from her, 'I wonder if you could think of anywhere I might find out something about Velda Turner – in London, perhaps?'

'I thought you had been watching her in London?'

'Not all the time. As I said, we were aware of the lady. But you may know more about – well, music hall, perhaps.'

'I know very little about music hall as I've never performed in it,' said Dorinda. I do know a little about what we do – that is to say, Will and I and some of the others – in the winter. Perhaps you could ask the Concert Artistes' Association.'

'The – what?'

'Concert Artistes' Association. It's quite new, only a few years old, but it has a list of members who are all professional artistes. I'm a member myself. Perhaps Velda was.'

'I've never heard of it, but if she was a member – and it would surprise me if she was – it wouldn't be under the name Velda Turner.'

'I wish, Mr Colyer,' said Dorinda sharply, 'you would tell me a little of what you already know about this woman. You ask me all sorts of personal questions and give me no answers. If I knew a little more I could probably help you.'

'Miss Alexander, I sincerely wish I could tell you more.'

'Very well.' Dorinda bowed slightly. 'Good morning, Inspector. Good hunting.'

'Miss Alexander.' The Inspector tipped his hat. And then turned back. 'May I ask – what was the name of the young man who captured your attention?'

Dorinda hesitated, then shrugged. 'Peter Prince,' she said. 'If it matters.'

'It might.' The Inspector gave her his lopsided grin and strode back along Victoria Place.

Maude was hovering in the foyer of The Alexandria.

'What did he want?'

'More questions. He wasn't satisfied about the whole diamond necklace thing.'

'But he knows you didn't steal it!'

'He wanted to know who reported that I had.'

'Oh.' Maude's hand went to her mouth. 'What did you tell him?'

'I told him Mr Shepherd had. And then he wanted to know why I joined the Wanderers.'

'He asked both those questions yesterday,' said Maude.

'And because we didn't answer them, he asked again.'

'And what did you say?'

'I told him I fell for Peter Prince.'

Maude frowned. 'Ah.'

'And he wanted know his name.'

'Oh dear.'

'Yes. So he may well go and look for him. Especially as I was foolish enough to tell him about the CAA.'

'Is Peter a member?'

'I've no idea. Will might know.' Dorinda went into the office and removed her jacket and hat. 'Now I need to start rehearsing. Any of the others here yet?'

'They all are,' said Maude. 'That Aramantha was moaning because you'd asked them to be early and you weren't here yourself.'

Dorinda laughed. 'Did you tell her I was being questioned by the police?'

'No!' Maude looked shocked.

'I will, then.' Dorinda made her way through the auditorium and clapped her hands.

75

'Good morning everybody!' she called out. 'I'm very sorry I wasn't here to meet you but,' she saw Aramantha open her mouth and held up a hand, 'I was being questioned by the police again.'

There was an outraged muttering.

'It's all right, the inspector wanted to know if any of us might have had any knowledge of what Velda Turner got up to in London in the winter.'

'How do we know she was in London in the winter?' said Phoebe reasonably.

'That's right, we don't,' said Algy. 'She could have been anywhere.'

'I did suggest he asked the CAA. Most of us are members, aren't we? Aramantha?'

'What's that when it's at 'ome?'

The others all looked at her in astonishment. 'The Concert Artistes' Association,' said Will. 'How do you get work in the winter? Most of ours comes through the members list.'

'What's that then?'

'A list of members that's supplied to people who wish to book someone for a concert or a Smoker.'

'Or an At Home,' put in Maisie. 'I do those – singing, you know.'

'Oh.' Aramantha shrugged. Everyone waited for her to say more but she remained silent.

'Ladies, let's start with the fairy song. We only need a little rearrangement of that one.' Dorinda climbed on stage and rehearsals began.

At lunchtime, Ted, Algy and Will went to remove the "cancelled" notices from the posters and came back to report that the news of Velda's death was all over town and it looked as though there would be standing room only at the early performance.

'Why, though?' said Dorinda when Maude told her this, delivering a hot pie for her lunch. 'It's not as if her ghost is going to appear.'

'People are like that. You know the way if there's a smash up in the Strand people will stand and gawp? Same thing.'

Dorinda shuddered. 'I hate it. I keep remembering that her body was found only just behind us here.' She thought for a moment. 'And that seems odd, doesn't it? Why here?'

'I don't know. Why not?'

'Well,' said Dorinda, 'she'd gone home, hadn't she? She'd spoken to me, telling the others to go on ahead, then we saw her go up the slope. When and why did she come back?'

'Forgot something?'

'She couldn't get in.'

They looked at each other. 'That's it!' said Dorinda. 'She was trying to get back in!'

'Or she saw someone trying to get back in,' said Maude.

'Yes, but that would mean she'd come here for another reason. No, I think she was trying to get in for some purpose.'

Maude frowned. 'Do you think you ought to tell the police?'

'I don't think they'd take that much notice of anything I said.'

'That Scotland Yard inspector would, I bet,' said Maude slyly.

'Why?' Dorinda looked startled.

'Quite handsome, isn't he?'

'Quite good looking, I suppose,' said Dorinda, taking a hasty bite of her pie.

'Lovely brown eyes.'

Dorinda, her mouth full, nodded.

'And curly dark hair.' Maude grinned. 'And quite the gent.'

Dorinda tried to speak and choked on a mouthful of crumbs.

Later, changed into her Pierrot costume, Dorinda peered out of the office window and saw the long queue all the way up the slope and along Victoria Place.

'We'd better open up, Maude, otherwise we'll be accused of clogging up the prom.' She sat down at the desk while Maude went to open up and take the money. The ghoulish nature of the British public still appalled her, however good it was for business. She tried not to think about poor Velda, or whoever she was, lying outside the back of the theatre all night. And that was odd, if you thought about it. If she'd been there all night, why had someone not seen her earlier? It was quite late in the morning when those screams had started. Was it only yesterday? Dorinda sighed and stood up. She didn't want to go outside until all her audience were seated, and she was restless.

The office door opened and in walked the unwelcome figure of Inspector Malkin.

'Inspector! I'm just about to – '

'I know that, Miss Alexander. But I have a few more questions.' Malkin, it appeared, was on a mission – and this time, he didn't have Inspector Colyer to restrain him.

Chapter Eleven

'Well, well, well!' interrupted a new voice. 'Hello, Dolly, me old mate! Entertaining a copper now, are we?'

Ivy, Lady Anderson strolled into the office behind Inspector Malkin, who whirled round as fast as his bulk would allow.

Ivy threw back her fashionable cape and stood, hands on her hips, displaying on her generous breast all the magnificence of the Anderson diamonds.

'Inspector – may I present Lady Anderson? Oh, and Sir Frederick.' Sir Frederick, looking mightily amused, had come quietly into the office behind his wife. Inspector Malkin's eyes bulged.

'Inspector.' Sir Frederick nodded towards the other man. 'I can't say I'm delighted to meet you, but perhaps it saves time? Miss Alexander has been a friend of my family's for some years – I thought perhaps we should reassure you of that.'

'Thank you, sir,' mumbled the inspector. 'I – er – I was just…' He stopped and gulped. 'I'll bid you good day.'

Ivy and Sir Frederick stood aside for him as he lumbered out of the office and Dorinda sank down in her office chair.

'How did you come to be here at the right moment?' she asked.

'We decided to come this morning. May and Ellen are here too,' said Ivy.

'We were in the queue when Maude noticed us and started waving,' said Sir Frederick.

'We had to push past everyone else – who didn't like

it – and when we got here Maude told us that fat inspector had gone into your office.' Ivy looked round. 'Not very cosy.'

'Do you think we did any good, my dear?' asked Sir Frederick.

Dorinda smiled a little tremulously. 'I'm sure you did. And now I had better go and take my place at the piano.'

'And we'd better find out seats, Freddie.' Ivy took him by the arm. 'Maude was sending May and Ellen to save us two of the best.'

Dorinda was surprised to receive a smattering of applause as she walked through the auditorium to take her seat, and understood when she saw May and Ellen clapping enthusiastically in the second row behind Ivy and Sir Frederick in the front row. She bowed slightly to the audience and took her seat. At her opening chord, the Alexandrians filed on to the stage in time honoured procession, lining up to sing the opening song, which was followed by Ted and Algy's cross talk act. After which, the show proceeded smoothly, as if one of their number hadn't suddenly been murdered the day before.

In the interval, Dorinda joined the company backstage.

'Going well,' said Will.

'Marvellous audience,' said Algy.

'Is that young Ivy in the front row?' asked Ted.

'It is, and Sir Freddie sitting next to her,' said Dorinda.

'And May and Ellen behind,' said Will.'

'Thought so,' said Ted.

'Who are they?' asked Maisie.

'Friends of Dorinda's,' said Will.

'A "sir"?' said Aramantha. ''Ow come?'

Will, Ted and Algy glared at her.

'Sorry, I'm sure,' she said, and turned her back on the company.

It was obvious that the other girls were also itching to know, but wisely, they said nothing.

Maude suddenly appeared round the curtain that separated the two dressing rooms from the area between them.

'Did you see who was in the audience?' she whispered.

'Sir Fred,' said Will.

'No, not him! That inspector again.'

'Oh, no,' groaned Dorinda. 'I thought Sir Freddie had got rid of him.'

'Not him, either – the other one,' said Maude. 'The good looking London one.'

Everyone looked at Dorinda.

'I expect he wants to see what Velda used to do,' said Phoebe hesitantly, and Dorinda threw her a grateful look.

'That'll be it, girl,' said Ted, clapping Phoebe on the back and nearly knocking her off her stool.

'Shall we get back to work, then?' suggested Will.

'Give them five more minutes,' said Dorinda. 'They haven't had long.'

When she returned to the piano, she cast a swift eye over the audience and spotted Jack Colyer straight away. Near the back, he was leaning against the wall, eyes fixed on her. Dorinda's stomach swooped and she looked quickly back at the keyboard. To her annoyance, she was aware of him all the way through the second half, but didn't once look in his direction again until the end when she turned to fact the audience to take her bow and saw that he was no longer there.

Aware of an inappropriate disappointment, she made her way out of the auditorium and into the foyer.

'Maude,' she called, 'when Sir Freddie and Ivy come out will you ask them to come into the office?'

Maude looked up from behind her little counter. 'That inspector's already in there,' she said with another sly smile.

'Oh, bother the man!' said Dorinda. 'I wanted to change.'

'I shall wait out here then.' The inspector's smooth voice made her jump. 'I apologise – *again*, Miss Alexander.'

Dorinda nodded, coolly, she hoped. 'I have friends in the audience this evening, Inspector. I was hoping to go to supper with them.'

'I hope you will.' He nodded and took up a position by Maude's counter. 'I believe I hear your audience coming out.'

Dorinda dived into her office and pulled her battered screen across a corner of the room as she began to peel off her costume.

Following a discreet tap on the door, she heard Ellen's voice asking if she could come in.

'Oh, yes, Ellen, do!' Dorinda put her head round the screen. 'I have to battle with this by myself normally – it would be lovely to have help.'

Ellen bustled in and shut the office door behind her.

'The others are all talking to some policeman out there. Not the first one, this is another one.'

'Yes.' Dorinda sighed. 'That's the Scotland Yard man. He couldn't be more different from the other one.'

'Looks all right.' Ellen dropped the flannel skirt over Dorinda's head.

'Mmm,' mumbled Dorinda, glad of the stuffy material hiding her hot face. This was getting ridiculous.

'There now,' said Ellen, tucking strands of Dorinda's hair into a hastily achieved pompadour. 'Stick on your hat. Sir Freddie's taking us all to supper.'

'Oh, I was going to suggest we ate together,' said Dorinda, equilibrium restored. 'How lovely.' She adjusted her hat and jacket, cast a quick look round the office, turned down the gas and ushered Ellen out into the foyer.

'Ah, Dorinda, my dear!' Sir Frederick came forward, took her hand and kissed it. 'You are a clever woman.'

'And blo – very talented,' said Ivy, kissing her cheek.

82

'Lovely show.'

'My I add my congratulations, Miss Alexander?' Inspector Colyer moved into the centre of the little group.

'It's the performers who are talented,' said Dorinda. 'I simply put them together.'

'And play all the way through,' said Ivy. 'You're as good as any of them.'

'I agree,' said Sir Frederick. 'Now, we're all going to supper, as soon as Will joins us. You will excuse us, Inspector?'

Inspector Colyer, looking amused, bowed his assent just as Will emerged through the door.

'I shall have to wait until the whole audience have left, Sir Fred,' said Dorinda. 'I have to lock up.'

'Would you allow me to do that for you, Miss Alexander?'

Everyone turned to look at Colyer.

'After all, I am a policeman, and I can inspect the premises to make sure all is well. I'll deliver your key to you afterwards.'

'What an excellent idea,' said Sir Frederick. 'I have a table reserved at Batelli's. I hope that will not take you out of your way?'

'It will not.' Colyer accepted the keys reluctantly handed to him by Dorinda with a small smile.

'Come on, then,' said Ivy. 'I'm ready for my supper.'

The whole party trooped out, Dorinda last, looking over her shoulder to where Colyer stood watching the strange little group.

'Enjoy your meal, Miss Alexander.'

Dorinda stopped. 'I'm not sure about this … '

'I'm quite trustworthy.' He stepped forward and gave her a little push. 'Go.'

Batelli's was a little way along Victoria Place, a small restaurant patronised mainly by the residents of the many new boarding houses wanting a change from the landladies' cabbage and watery gravy. Batelli himself had come down from London in the wake of the railway and had gradually begun to introduce some of the cuisine of his home country to the suspicious natives of Nethergate. Luckily he was also adept at providing the favourite dishes of his adoptive country. Sir Frederick had discovered him when he had taken a large house on Cliff Terrace, and now he lived permanently in the area visited frequently with his wife. His maid and cook, however had never been and were as excited as children at Christmas.

'Isn't this grand, Dolly?' whispered Ellen, as they were shown to a large round table set with sparkling glasses and shiny cutlery.

Dorinda was amused. 'You see the dining room at the Place like this all the time, though, Ellen.'

Ellen shook her head. 'Not much, these days. They don't entertain, see? The county don't approve. We get it up nice for Christmas and Easter when the boys are home, but that's about it. I feel that sorry for Mrs Nemone.'

'Why didn't she come with you tonight?'

'She was asked. But you know what she's like. Just smiled and said "no thank you". Course, Miss Julia wanted to come, and Ivy and Sir Fred would have brought her, but Mrs Nemone said 'no'.

'So are the coppers going to let you alone now, Dolly?' Ivy called across the table.

'I've no idea. They're still trying to find out all they can about Velda, but none of us know anything, do we?' Dorinda appealed to Will and Maude.

'Except she said she worked at the old Britannia before the fire,' said Maude.

'The Britannia, heh?' said Ivy, looking thoughtful.

'When was the fire?' asked Will. '1900?'

'Yes, just after the last pantomime,' said Ivy. Everyone looked at her in surprise. She grinned round the table. 'My sister was in the chorus of the pantomime. I saw it about a

84

dozen times. If your Velda was in it, Ada will know.'

'I didn't know you had a sister, Ivy,' said Dorinda.

'No reason why you should. She came to the wedding though, which you wouldn't, if I remember rightly.'

'I couldn't really, could I?' said Dorinda, going pink. Sir Frederick cleared his throat and everyone became very busy with their plates and napkins.

'Anyway, I'll write and ask her,' said Ivy. 'Shame we haven't got one of them telephones. We must get one, Freddie.'

'Who will we have though to call?' asked Sir Frederick. 'Your sister wouldn't have one.'

'That's true.' Ivy was looking thoughtful again. 'But we could pay for her to have one, couldn't we? It'd be nice to talk to her more often.'

'You've lived away from your family since you were thirteen, Ivy,' said May.

'Don't mean I don't miss 'em, does it? I'll write tomorrow, Dolly.'

Batelli himself appeared behind Sir Frederick and leant over to whisper in his ear. Sir Frederick pointed to Dorinda. Batelli beamed, and trotted round the table.

'Your keys, madame.' He bowed, and handed her the bunch of keys. 'A gentleman delivered them.'

'Oh!' Dorinda took the keys. 'Is he still here?'

'Oh, no, madame. He just delivered the keys.'

'There, Dolly. Good as his word, wasn't he?' said Maude.

'Yes.' Dorinda stared at the keys as if they could give her some answers. 'But he's been quite a long time about it, hasn't he?'

'He'll have searched the theatre while no one was there,' said Will.

'How horrible.'

'Not at all,' said Sir Frederick. 'The man's trying to find a murderer. And hasn't Sherlock Holmes said

85

somewhere that the clue to the murderer lies with the victim?'

'If he didn't say it, he should have,' said Ivy. 'And if that Mr Detective can do it, so can we. I'll write to Ada tomorrow. And what we ought to do, Dolly, is have a nice little visit up to London to see what we can find out.'

Chapter Twelve

An argument was going on in the office of The Alexandria the following morning.

'We don't take days off, Will,' said Dorinda. 'And particularly not me. I play for you all.'

'I'm sure we can find someone to fill in,' said Maude. 'You ought to go with Ivy – see what you can find out. This business is going to hang over us until the murderer's found.'

'I don't see what good going to London is going to do.'

'You talk to Ivy's sister Ada, and if she's still in the business you can ask around. Pity we haven't got any pictures of Velda.'

'Aramantha wanted us to have some postcards done. I said we couldn't afford it.'

'Ah! You can also ask about Aramantha,' said Will. 'We don't know much about her, either, do we?'

'I still don't see how I can go,' said Dorinda stubbornly.

'I'm going to go and find Mickey Bennett and ask if he knows any pianists.' Will stood and jammed his hat on his head.

'He doesn't use a pianist,' said Dorinda.

'I know, but he knows an awful lot of people, does Mickey. I'll see you later.'

Dorinda looked helplessly at Maude. 'I really can't go, you know.'

'I really think you should. That Scotland Yard inspector's cleverer than the other one, but he don't know where to look.' Maude folded her arms under her bosom and looked serious.

'I think he does, because he's been watching her. Perhaps not him personally, but he said "they" were aware of her. That means the police. And I really want to know why.' Dorinda scowled at her desk. 'I feel so angry that someone who was a common criminal should have come here under false pretences.'

'We don't know she was a common criminal,' said Maude, 'but there you are. You're angry and you want to know why. So you *should* go to London with Ivy.'

Will came back looking despondent.

'Mickey doesn't know anyone who could help. He said if he did he'd book him for the *Magic Minstrels*, and did we still have that old piano on wheels.'

'Did you tell him we were still using it?' asked Maude.

'I did.' Will sighed and sat down on the edge of Dorinda's desk. 'All he could offer us was a piano accordion.'

'I told you I wouldn't be able to go,' said Dorinda.

'We could always close for a couple of days,' said Maude.

Will and Dorinda stared at her in shock.

'Well, why not? We've already closed for one day. And it isn't as if it's July or August, is it?'

'Could we?' Dorinda looked at Will. 'Would the others mind?'

'Not as long as they got paid,' said Will. 'They'd get a little holiday.'

'As soon as Ivy tells us what she hears from her sister, I'll say we can go,' said Dorinda. 'At least I've got a couple of days to think about it.'

Jack Colyer turned up again after the afternoon performance.

'I thought I ought to tell you I found nothing last night,' he said, his eyes on Dorinda's hair, which having been released from under her Pierrot hat, was tumbling down her back.

'What do you mean, you found nothing? Were you looking for something?'

'You must have realised I would take the opportunity to have a good look round – especially in the ladies' dressing room.'

'We did wonder,' said Dorinda. 'Don't you have to ask permission to do that?'

'You had given me the keys. I considered I had permission.'

'What did you expect to find?'

'I hoped I might find some evidence of what Velda Turner was doing here.'

'Why? She left nothing in the dressing room except her costumes. And only one of those was her own – the evening dress.'

'And a very nice one, too.'

'Was there nothing in the room she shared with Maisie?'

'I've been unable to look at that. Malkin had that searched.'

'Oh, dear. Poor Maisie.'

Colyer smiled. 'Indeed.

'You still won't tell me why you were watching her in London?'

'I didn't actually say she was being watched. I said we were aware of her.'

'As what? Was she a prostitute?'

Colyer looked shocked. 'Miss Alexander!'

Dorinda sighed in exasperation. 'Inspector Colyer, surely you don't imagine a woman in my position knows nothing about that world? I live in it, sir!'

She had never seen Colyer at a loss in their short acquaintance, but it was apparent that she had taken the wind out of his sails.

'I suppose I should tell you that Lady Anderson and I

are going to London shortly. We shall close The Alexandria for a few days.'

'Why?'

Dorinda's eyebrows rose. 'Is that any of your business? I'm simply having the courtesy to inform you that I would not be available until I return. As I am not sure when we leave, neither am I sure when I shall return.'

'I suppose this visit would not be in order to make your own enquiries?'

'We are to visit Lady Anderson's sister.'

'And where might she be?'

'If you mean where does she live, I'm not precisely sure.'

'And no one else in London? Will you be visiting your old school, perhaps?'

'Why would you think that? I am not going to visit anybody else as far as I know.' And that was true, Dorinda thought. She didn't know.

There was a pause. Colyer turned towards the door, then turned back.

'What happened to the Shepherd family after you left to join the Pierrots?'

Dorinda's breath caught in her throat.

'Wha –what do you mean, what happened?'

'What did they do? After Mr Earnest Shepherd accused you of stealing the necklace?'

Dorinda stared at him, her brain racing.

'I didn't tell you that,' she said slowly.

'No. Malkin was very thorough. Why he has such a desire to lock you up I have no idea, but he went through every piece of information he could find, which led at last to a retired office called Barrett. He remembered the event very well. Quite amused by it, apparently. Remembered having to escort Mr Shepherd away after Lady Ivy displayed the famous diamonds. Much as she did last night, it seems.'

'Yes,' said Dorinda, wondering what else she should say.

'Mr Shepherd doesn't appear to live with the family at Anderson Place.' Colyer was watching her carefully.

Dorinda swallowed. 'No.'

'Do you know where he is?'

'Of course not!'

'You are very close to the family. I thought you would know.'

'I worked for them,' said Dorinda. 'So did Ivy. They were kind to us.'

'And she married Sir Frederick. Cause a scandal, did it?'

'I wouldn't know.'

'Really? Yet you stayed here in Nethergate and they moved to Anderson Place. Why didn't you know?'

'They didn't move to Anderson Place immediately. They went back to London at the end of the season.'

'Do they still have a house in London?'

'I believe so.' Dorinda pulled herself together. 'I find these questions extremely intrusive.'

'Murder is intrusive,' said Colyer.

'What has this to do with the murder?'

'I don't know.' Colyer's mouth lifted in his lopsided grin. 'Malkin seems sure it does have something to do with it.'

'Well, it's perfectly ridiculous. What could the Andersons or the Shepherds have to do with the death of a chorus girl in London?'

'She died here, not in London.'

'I meant from London, of course.' Dorinda stood up. 'If you don't mind, I have to send out for food before the evening performance.'

'Of course.' Colyer bowed. 'Enjoy your trip to London.'

Dorinda watched him out for the door, then went and

91

locked it.

'Was that the inspector again?' Maude came up behind her. 'What did he want this time?'

'He came to tell me he found nothing in the theatre last night. He searched, apparently.'

'Cheek!' gasped Maude.

'He's a policeman,' said Dorinda wearily, 'and I *had* given him my keys. What do you expect him to do?'

'I don't know, I'm sure,' said Maude doubtfully.

'I told him I was going to London.'

'Why did you do that?'

'Because he might want to speak to me, and if he finds The Alexandria closed again, he'll think I've run away again.' Dorinda went back into her office and sank on to her chair with her head in her hands. 'Oh, Maude. And then he asked about Mr Shepherd.'

'He *what*?' gasped Maude.

'I know. He was asking questions about the family. I didn't know what to say.'

'But why is he asking? It hasn't got anything to do with Velda. It was years ago and she only arrived a few weeks ago.'

'Not that many years,' said Dorinda. 'And I asked the same question. He said Malkin feels sure I'm involved in some way. I wish I knew why. How could I be?'

'I think Malkin resents you because you're a woman in business and successful.' Maude pulled up the other chair. 'I don't think there's anything more than that. He just saw you'd been accused of theft and that was enough for him.'

'I don't suppose he wants women to get the vote, then, do you?' Dorinda pulled a face. 'What do you think, Maudie? Why was she killed?'

'I think it was something to do with her life in London. I think she was running away from something.'

'But what? And was it the same reason Scotland Yard was "aware" of her?'

'That's what you and Ivy are going to find out,' said Maud. 'And now we need to get something to eat. I'll get me hat.'

Ivy, followed by Julia Shepherd, burst into the foyer the following morning.

'Morning, Dolly, morning, Maude.' She flopped down on one of the gilt chairs provided for audience members overcome by heat or alcohol during the shows. 'Ada don't know the name, but says why don't we go up for a day or so and see what we can find out. She's going to speak to a couple of the girls who was at The Britannia. Did you talk her into it, Maudie?'

'Yes, she did.' Dorinda laughed. 'We're going to close for a couple of days as we can't find another pianist.'

'Oh, I could have –' began Julia, but the three women shouted her down.

'Most definitely not something your mother would allow. Highly unsuitable,' said Dorinda. 'But how did you hear so soon, Ivy?'

'You know how quick the post is now? I reckon Ada must've got my letter in the evening, and wrote back straight away, so I got hers this morning. When can you get away?'

'Tomorrow?' suggested Dorinda. 'I can't go today – I've got to give everyone notice that they've got a holiday. And I must be back for Saturday.'

'It's Wednesday now!' said Ivy. 'Two days ain't going to give us much time.'

'Can't help it,' said Dorinda. 'I can't possibly miss the weekend trade.'

'Go today,' urged Maude. 'We'll tell the others, and perhaps we can give this afternoon's audience a spot of the old Will's Wanderers without accompaniment.'

'Oh, well done, Maude!' said Ivy.

Dorinda looked doubtful. 'I don't know. The girls don't know the old stuff.'

'It's easy enough to learn,' said Maude. 'Now go on, go back to the digs and pack your things.

'We've got the car,' said Ivy proudly, 'so we'll go by your place first for you to pick up what you need, then we'll drop Julia off at The Place and go on to the station in Canterbury.'

'I'll go and talk to Will,' said Maude.

'I'll come too,' said Dorinda, still feeling worried. In the end they all trooped through the auditorium to find Will on the stage mending props.

'No, Maude's right, Dolly,' he said. 'You need to go. Because I've been thinking. We've forgotten about that woman who tried to say one of us had stolen her necklace, haven't we?'

'You didn't mention this. What about her?' said Ivy.

'That was against you, Dolly. Didn't strike me at first, but don't you think it was a bit strange, coming to you to ask about a stolen necklace? Exactly what you'd been accused of doing the same thing three years ago?'

Chapter Thirteen

Dorinda gaped.

'Gawd!' said Ivy.

'What does it mean?' asked Maude.

'I don't know what it means,' said Will. 'It just looks suspicious to me. Especially as the woman ran off. No one's seen her since, have they?'

'But why would someone be after me?' said Dorinda in a shaky voice.

'For the same reason that Inspector Malkin doesn't like you?' suggested Maude. 'Because you're a successful woman?'

'Who's here that remembers you from three years ago?' asked Ivy. 'What about that *Magic Minstrels* lot?'

'Mickey would never do anything like that!' said Will, shocked.

'Besides, he thinks he gets more business,' said Maude. 'Before there were two sets of minstrels on the beach and folk thought if they'd seen one they'd seen them both. We're different, so they go and see both. And we're inside, and he's outside. People have to pay up front for our shows, but he still bottles.'

'Who else?' said Ivy.

'The policeman who was there that time. They found him. His name was Barrett,' said Dorinda.

'Why would he do anything like that?' said Maude.

'Inspector Colyer said he was amused by the memory.'

'Daddy,' said Julia in a small voice.

The other three turned to look at her, almost forgotten,

standing behind Maude.

'What?' said Will.

'That policeman. I remember, because I was there with Mama. Daddy was angry and the policeman thought it was funny when Ivy showed him the necklace. It was, a bit. But I was scared.'

Ivy drew the girl close to her. 'You should never have had to see that.'

'No,' agreed Julia. 'But I was used to Daddy shouting. It was much quieter when he wasn't here.'

The adults exchanged glances.

'I think it's time we took you home,' said Ivy. 'Your mother will scold me.'

'She can't tell you off now,' said Julia, with a giggle, and there was an audible sigh of relief at this return to normal. But as Will followed Dorinda through the auditorium, he whispered: 'It couldn't be him, could it?'

'Mr Shepherd? The murderer?' Dorinda stopped dead, eyes wide.

'No! The person behind the break in and the false thieving claim. He'd try and break you, if he could. He thinks you were the one who turned Mrs Nemone against him.'

'He managed that himself,' said Dorinda bitterly, 'but yes, you're right, it could be. But I haven't seen him in town.'

'He'd take care not to be seen, wouldn't he? Or he'd pay someone to do it.'

'But not Velda.'

'I don't think Velda's death has anything to do with us,' said Will. 'It's something to do with Velda's past.'

'Oi! I've just remembered.' Reaching the foyer, Ivy turned suddenly. 'I found a picture.'

'Actually, I found it,' said Julia.

'She was being nosy,' said Ivy fondly.

'A picture? Of what?' asked Dorinda.

'Of all of you,' said Julia. 'It called you "The Alexandrians".'

'Oh, in *The Mercury*!' said Will. 'Remember when that Cecil came to see us the day we opened? With that enormous camera.'

'It wasn't a very good photograph,' sniffed Julia.

'Well, it had been printed in the paper,' said Maude. 'I don't expect it looked that bad at first.'

'That was very clever of you,' said Dorinda. 'Why did you look for it?'

'I wanted to see what the girl looked like. The one who's dead.'

'Little ghoul!' said Dorinda.

'So we're going to take it up to Ada. See if she might recognise anyone.'

Julia sniffed again. 'I don't suppose she will. I could only just recognise Dorinda, Maude and Will and I know them *very* well.'

'We can try,' said Ivy. 'Come on now. Maude, Will – thanks for this. Dolly'll be grateful one day!'

'I am grateful.' Dorinda leant forward and kissed Maude's cheek. Will gave her a swift hug and handed her her hat and bag. 'Safe journey,' he said.

At the top of the slope, watched over by Billy the odd job man, now resplendent in a mechanic's uniform, stood a black and claret coloured motor car. The hood was up at the back, but Ivy still handed a scarf to Dorinda.

'Tie it over your hat, Doll. Gets a bit breezy. Got yours on, Julia?'

Julia had, also a long buttoned up overcoat. Ivy donned the same sort of garment and Billy handed them all gallantly into the vehicle.

'You'll have to pick up a coat at your lodgings, Dolly,' said Ivy. 'Drive slow, Billy, so Miss Dorinda don't get too cold.

Dorinda hadn't given much thought to riding in a motor

car and suddenly realised she was scared. She watched as Billy swung the handle, getting rather red in the face, and noticed the increasing throng of holiday makers who stopped to watch. She shrank back between Ivy and Julia.

'Noting to be frightened of, Dorinda,' said Julia. 'It's really rather exciting. I'm going to drive a car when I grow up.'

'You?' Dorinda was shocked.

'Of course! I should have thought you would, too, being what Grandpa calls an "independent woman".'

'Women don't drive!'

'Of course they do, Dolly,' laughed Ivy. 'Look out, we're off!'

Billy had regained the driver's seat and with a good deal of rattling and the odd mild explosion, they were indeed off. At first, Dorinda kept her eyes closed, but when she opened them she realised that the world wasn't rushing past at an incredible speed, in fact they were moving more slowly than a railway carriage. She sat up, keeping a hand to her head to keep her hat from disappearing, and immediately got a faceful of dust.

'That's why we keep the scarf over our face,' said Ivy. 'Here we are, this is your place, isn't it? Julia and me'll wait here.'

Dorinda swiftly packed a small valise with a few garments for two days stay in London, found her heaviest winter coat and a chiffon evening stole to cover her hat and face, and ran back to the motor car.

'That's just the thing,' Ivy approved. 'Hop in.'

Billy jumped down to assist Dorinda into the vehicle and they set off towards Anderson Place.

'Does Ada know we're coming?' Dorinda asked.

'I wrote as soon as I got her letter, so she'll have that this afternoon. Bloody miracle the post, isn't it?'

'And you really think she'll be able to help?'

Ivy shrugged. 'Don't know. But if we can find anything

out about your Velda it'll set your mind at rest, won't it?'

'I'm not so sure about that,' said Dorinda, 'but I suppose if we find something that could be the reason for her murder, at least I won't feel as if it's my fault.'

'Come on, Dolly. How can it be your fault? Will's right. The things that have happened at The Alexandria look like someone who's local – or at least was here three years ago. Velda ain't – hasn't – got anything to do with that.' Ivy's vocabulary slipped now and again.

Sir Frederick, Mrs Shepherd, May and Ellen all came out to greet them, the two maids, Connie and Edie, hovering behind, once again in their black and white afternoon uniforms. Ivy had obviously anticipated the immediate departure for London, for Ellen handed her a valise, much smarter than Dorinda's and Sir Frederick passed a folded newspaper to Dorinda.

'You'll find the photograph in there,' he said. 'Not very clear, but it may help.'

Amidst a flurry of good wishes for a successful journey, the motor car, having had its insides attended to briefly by Billy, set off again towards Canterbury.

'Makes life a lot easier,' said Ivy with satisfaction. 'Even if we do keep getting punctures.'

However, the journey to the railway station was accomplished without incident, and Billy waited with them to hand them into a first class carriage when the up train arrived self-importantly in a whoosh of steam.

'I do love a train journey,' said Ivy, who seemed to be relishing the whole adventure.

'You seem to be loving everything,' said Dorinda, amused.

'Course I am. I told you the other day, I get so bored. I don't know how these county ladies do it. They don't do anything for themselves. Do you know, when I went with Nemone to call on some old biddies, one of them dropped a handkerchief and didn't even pick it up! She just glared at this poor little maid, who in the end realised what she wanted and went to pick it up for her. Shocking! At least Nemone never treated us like that. And no one treats Connie and Edie like it, either. *And* we call 'em by their own names.'

'Their own names?'

'Well some of 'em, you know, they just call all the maids Jane and all the footmen James. Can't be bothered to be civil.'

Dorinda shook her head. 'No wonder when they get time off they want to have fun.'

'They never get no time off,' said Ivy. 'I couldn't stand it. Didn't realise how lucky I was to get taken on by Nemone.'

'Why wasn't she like that?' Dorinda was curious.

'I don't know. Course, I didn't know her ma, but I expect it was something to do with her. It was a love match, you know.'

'Sir Fred and his first wife?'

'Yes. She wasn't what you'd call top drawer, either. Oh, not like me, but she came from trade or something. I expect she'd not been brought up to boss servants around.'

'Well, we all did well out of being taken on by Nemone, I suppose.'

Ivy turned to look at her friend in astonishment. '*You* say that? Gawd, Dolly, you're a piece!'

Dorinda felt her cheeks turning red again. 'In the end, I have, haven't I? I've got the theatre. Pavilion. All thanks to Sir Fred.'

'You didn't 'arf pay the price, though,' said Ivy.

Dorinda was silent for a moment. 'You don't think there was anything in what Julia said, do you?'

'About him? Wouldn't be surprised. Good job she didn't say any more, though, wasn't it?'

'How much do you think she really knows?'

'As much as anyone outside the family,' said Ivy.

'Nothing.'

'She was there ...' said Dorinda, looking uncomfortable.

'You were ill,' said Ivy firmly. 'We looked after you.'

'I've been so worried about the girls in the company getting to hear about it. Or anybody else.'

'Nobody's going to talk, Dolly. And it beats me why you should be worried.'

'Ivy, you know perfectly well my reputation would be ruined.'

'Quite makes me want to run off and join those suffrage women,' said Ivy. 'Didn't ruin his reputation, did it?'

'Actually, it didn't do him any good,' said Dorinda. 'He's still got the town house, but everyone must wonder why the family isn't there.'

'Don't you worry about Mr Earnest Shepherd, my girl. If he ain't – hasn't – got his just desserts yet, it won't be long before he has.'

'What do you mean?' asked Dorinda, alarmed.

'Just he's bound to put a foot wrong sooner or later. There'll be another girl, and this time it won't be hushed up.'

'It was hushed up for my sake,' said Dorinda, 'not his, and I'm so grateful.'

'Brought shame on the family, that's what he did,' said Ivy robustly. 'Shouldn't have got away with it.'

'He was made to look foolish that time with the necklace, though,' said Dorinda, with a faint smile.

'And he did that out of revenge, didn't he? So what young Julia says might be right. He hates you, all right.'

London was as dirty and noisy as Dorinda remembered. The last time she'd been here was to hire Maisie and Phoebe for The Alexandrians, but now it was summer, and the air was thick and heavy, the smells more penetrating. Ivy approached a cab, and gave the address. The cabbie

101

looked as if he wasn't too pleased about having to drive all the way from Victoria to Hoxton, but nevertheless flicked his tired horse into movement and they plodded into the press of traffic.

Dorinda was surprised to pull up outside a neat terrace of houses on the north side of a quiet square.

Ivy grinned. 'Not at all like the slums round here. I was able to do Ada a bit of good, thanks to my old darling.'

On the front steps a woman slightly younger than Ivy, attended by a small girl who clung to her leg, was waiting to greet them.

'Lovely to meet you, Miss Dolly,' she said, taking Dorinda's valise. 'Heard a lot about you.'

Dorinda looked quickly at Ivy, who gave a slight shake of her head.

'Now come and sit down. Tea's ready, and you'll want a bite to eat, won't you?"

Settled at the big kitchen table in the bright kitchen, Ivy got down to business and pulled out the newspaper.

'Now, Ada,' she said. 'It's not very good, but do you see anyone in this picture you recognise?'

Ada peered at the paper. After a moment she looked up, her eyes bright. 'Yes, I do!

'Good!' said Ivy with satisfaction. 'That one?'

Ada looked. 'Oh, no,' she said. 'That one,' and pointed at Aramantha.

Chapter Fourteen

Dorinda and Ivy gasped together.

'She was in the Britannia pantomime?' said Ivy.

'Yes, she was.' Ada sounded grim. 'And a right troublemaker she was, too.'

'And you don't know this one?' Ivy pointed at Velda, who, to be fair, was keeping her face averted as much as she could in the face of the photographer's demands.

Ada peered even more closely at the paper.

'It could be Martha,' she said doubtfully, 'but I can't be sure.'

'We knew her as Velda Turner,' said Dorinda. 'And Aramantha didn't recognise her when she turned up. Seemed to be jealous, in fact.'

'Can't be her, then,' said Ada. 'Martha and Edith were close. Too close, some said.'

Ivy and Dorinda looked at each other.

'Had they been in any other Britannia shows before the pantomime?' asked Dorinda.

'No, and I'd been in the chorus for – oh, any number of shows. They said they'd been doing the halls up north.'

'Together?' asked Ivy.

'That's what they said.'

'And this girl's name was Edith? No wonder she calls herself Aramantha,' said Ivy.

'Do you know anything about their background?' asked Dorinda. 'Or where they went when they left the Britannia?'

'I know where they should have gone,' said Ada darkly. 'Prison, that's where.'

103

'Why? What happened?' said Ivy.

'Fleeced some of the gentlemen, didn't they?' Ada sat back and folded her arms, a pillar of rectitude.

'How did they do that?' asked Dorinda.

'Well, you know as how some gentlemen like to take out the chorus girls?' Ada patted her hair self-consciously. 'Used to get took out quite regular meself, actually.'

'Yes, yes, we know that,' said Ivy impatiently. 'Tell us about Martha and Edith.'

'One day old Crauford – the boss, you know – he come into the dressing room. Very flustered he was. And he says this gentleman's here and wants to make a complaint.'

'Yes? Go on,' prompted Ivy.

'Well, this gentleman comes in and he's in a great taking on. And he points at Martha and says it's her.'

'What's her?' asked Dorinda.

'We didn't know, did we? And then he points at Edith and says she's in it, too.'

'Lord!' said Ivy. 'What did they do?'

'Nothing. Just stayed as still as statues. And Crauford asks them what they've got to say, and Edith says, all cocky like, 'Never seen him before.' So then the gentleman turns nasty and says he's bringing in the police, so Crauford hustles him out of the dressing room and says to Edith and Martha he'll speak to them later.'

'So what happened next?' asked Dorinda.

'We all asked Edith and Martha what was going on, and they both said nothing, they'd never seen him before and we carried on getting changed. And then they disappeared. Just didn't turn up for the next show. Course, we all thought they'd been done in, especially when it come out what they'd been doing.'

'What had they been doing?' asked Ivy.

'Martha – she was the prettiest one, see, and quiet, if you know what I mean? She'd go out with a gentleman if she thought he was rich enough, and after a bit she'd say yes to a nice supper somewhere private and – well, you know.' She looked down at her lap. 'And then when she'd got him where she wanted him, sort of, Edith would come in and steal his money and his watch. Only with this gentleman I told you about, he followed Martha afterwards and she went straight back to her lodgings and he sees her with Edith. And it turns out they'd been doing it for months, and probably did it wherever they'd been before.'

'Ah!' Ivy sat back with satisfaction. 'And that's what they were planning down in Nethergate, only they pretended not to know one another.'

Dorinda was frowning. 'But you don't get those sort of gentlemen at seaside concert parties,' she said. 'And there aren't any hotels where they could take girls to supper like the Savoy – in Nethergate. It isn't the same at all.'

'But that's why your Inspector Colyer said he was interested in her. It's a wonder he wasn't after Aramantha, too.'

'What exactly happened in Nethergate?' asked Ada. 'You didn't tell me.'

Between them, Dorinda and Ivy related the story of Velda's murder. 'And there were a couple of incidents before that, but I don't think they were anything to do with Velda,' said Dorinda.

'But they could be to do with Aramantha,' said Ivy.

'How? Why?' Dorinda was beginning to feel as if she was trapped in a spider's web. 'I don't understand.'

'The office – that could've been her, couldn't it?' said Ivy.

'No, she was out with the others – it was Saturday morning – changeover day.'

'Oh.' Ivy pursed her lips and frowned. 'Well, the old woman with the necklace, then. Suppose Aramantha really had nicked them pearls?'

'I don't see how,' said Dorinda. 'Someone would have noticed. All the attention was on the Serenaders.'

'Then it come out Edith – that's your Aramantha, ain't it? – was a dip, too,' said Ada.

'But even a good dip can't pull pearls from an old woman's neck when he – or she – is dressed up in a silver Pierrot costume with people close up round 'em,' said Ivy. 'No, you're right, Doll, she couldn't have been mixed up in it.'

Dorinda sighed. 'It takes us no further forward, does it? We know now – or think we know – why the police were aware of Velda. But that brings up more questions. If they – the police – knew where Velda was, and they did, because Inspector Colyer told me she lived in Clapham, why didn't they arrest her? And why weren't they aware of Aramantha too?'

'Perhaps they were,' said Ivy.

'But Colyer didn't recognise her when he came to The Alexandria,' objected Dorinda.

'But it was Martha who got the gentlemen interested,' said Ada. 'Edith only crept in at the last minute.'

'So not many people would have known about Edith?' said Ivy.

'Old Crauford, and the bloke who come to the theatre, and us girls, o'course.'

'But surely it was reported to the police?' said Dorinda.

'Only after they'd gone.'

'So the police wouldn't know about Edith?' said Ivy. 'That's why he didn't recognise her, Doll!'

'So,' mused Dorinda, 'did they both come to Nethergate to work together, or did they not know the other was there?'

'You said Aramantha – Edith – Gawd, this is confusing, come down because you found her up here. Her and that Phoebe, didn't you say?'

'Yes, they were working at a little hall off the Strand. I'd been talking to a couple of the Gaiety Girls who said there were two girls who'd come about an audition but

106

been turned away. But they'd been very good. So I tracked them down. The place off the Strand was awful. They both jumped at the chance of Nethergate.'

'And the other one – the one who was murdered – she just turned up days before you opened?'

'Velda, yes. Very ladylike, very talented and quiet. And seemed to like us. She was very concerned about the incidents in the theatre.'

'There!' said Ivy, looking satisfied. 'I'll lay a pound she didn't know the other one was there when she arrived, and suspected her of playing them tricks! And she was going to tip you off, but the other one bumped her off first.'

Dorinda looked doubtful and Ada eagerly interested.

'It's a theory,' said Dorinda.

'And it don't involve my family,' said Ivy. 'And that's what you were worried about.'

'Yes,' said Dorinda thankfully. 'But is it true?'

'I reckon your Inspector Colyer don't know nothing about Edith – Aramantha – so you better tell him,' said Ivy. 'Then he can look into her. She struck me as a bit of a madam on stage.'

'Oh, she is,' said Dorinda with a sigh. 'Always trying to upstage the other girls, although she didn't with Velda. She was very put out when I hired *her*. Very resentful.'

'There, see!' said Ivy triumphantly. 'Don't that go to prove what I said? After the business at The Britannia, they took off and had words, so they split up. And then after all that time the pair of them turn up at the same place, in a little out of the way seaside town. They must have been sick to find each other there.'

'Ada, would you be prepared to swear that was Edith in the picture?' asked Dorinda.

'I'd rather see 'er in the flesh, so to speak,' said Ada, with an eye on her big sister.

Ivy laughed. 'Go on with you. You come down and

spend some time with Freddie and me. I've told you, you're always welcome.'

'It don't seem right, some'ow, though,' said Ada. 'With the nobs.'

'You can stay downstairs with May and Ellen – you liked them, didn't you? Dolly knows us all, too. Say you'll come, you and the kids, and we can all go down to Nethergate and the kids can play on the sand.'

'What about my Tommy?'

'He can come, too,' said Ivy.

'No, he's got to work. He don't get no time off.'

'Well, he can do what the nobs do. Pop down at the weekend. Does he get Sunday off?'

'Yes,' said Ada cautiously, 'but he won't like it.'

'Why ever not?' asked Ivy.

'Because she won't be here to look after him,' said Dorinda. 'Where is he now, Ada?'

'He'll be at the Queen's Head.' Ada looked down into her lap. 'He's not a bad bloke. But …'

'You leave him to me,' said Ivy robustly. 'I'm going to sit up and wait for him. You can go on up to bed, Dolly.'

Ada wavered, then gave in. 'Come on, Miss – Dolly. Best to leave her to it when she sets her mind on summat.'

Dorinda agreed and followed Ada up the stairs to a little attic room.

'I'm sorry you 'as to share with Ivy, miss, but we ain't got no other rooms. Course, we're lucky to 'ave this 'ouse, thanks to Ivy and Sir Freddie, and the kiddies 'avin' their own rooms, like. Well, the girls share, and Bobby – well 'e's got 'is own room!' Ada said this with an air of wonder, which Dorinda found touching.

'This is lovely, Ada, and it's very kind of you to have us. You've been more help than you can imagine, and I think you deserve a little holiday by the sea. And you know it's Sir Freddie who helped me buy and build The Alexandria, don't you? He's a lovely man.'

108

''E is that, Miss.' Ada turned to go. 'Look, see, we've even got the electric in 'ere. You won't 'ave to bother with no candles.'

Ada took herself off and Dorinda sat on one of the narrow iron beds in the electric light and waited for Ivy to come and tell her what was going to happen next.

Chapter Fifteen

By the time Ivy came into the room, Dorinda was fast asleep on top of the covers. Ivy shook her awake.

'Sorted our Tommy out,' she said, unwinding pearls from her neck. 'Told him I'd pay for him to come down on the train on Sunday. He's all right really, just don't understand women.'

Dorinda sat up sleepily. 'Your sort of women,' she said. 'He understands his own sort, and they don't go off to the seaside with a baronet and his wife.'

'Time he learnt, then,' said Ivy. 'Get undressed and have a good sleep, now. We've got a train journey with three kids to make tomorrow.'

As it happened, the train journey was no problem at all. The only trains Ada and her children had used before were the Hop Pickers' Specials, run to take Londoners to the Hop Farms every September. This first class carriage completely overawed them, and for the most part they were silent, except for a few frightened squeakings from Ivy junior, aged two.

When they arrived in Canterbury, Dorinda was relieved to see that although Sir Frederick had driven the motor car to meet them, Billy had also brought the carriage.

'I thought Ada and the children would feel more comfortable in the carriage.' Sir Frederick handed his wife into the motor car. 'Will you come with us, Dorinda? Billy will take you on to Nethergate.'

'I wondered if Billy could take us all to Nethergate, Sir Fred. The children can see the sea, and I might be able to introduce Ada to – well, to the company.'

'They don't expect you back till tomorrow, Dolly. They won't be there.' Ivy paused in tying her scarf over her hat.

'Oh.' Dorinda looked doubtfully from Ada, loading children and boxes into the carriage to Sir Frederick and Ivy. 'Very well, I'll come with you.'

'What we'll do, see,' said Ivy, when they were settled in the motor, 'is we'll unload Ada and the kids at The Place, send you on to Nethergate, then later on I'll bring them down and we can meet you.'

'I hate to interfere with these arrangements,' said Sir Frederick, 'but would it not be advisable for Ada to be without the children when she meets this person?' Sir Frederick had been apprised of their arrival and the situation in the very expensive telegraph Ivy had sent him that morning.

His wife regarded him thoughtfully. 'That's not a bad idea, Freddie.'

'I agree,' said Dorinda. 'What do we do, then? Wait until tomorrow?'

'Might be best.' Ivy nodded and patted Sir Frederick's shoulder. 'Proper wise old darling, isn't he?'

At Anderson Place, Ada and the children were unloaded and given over to the care of May and Ellen, who were delighted, Dorinda paid a fleeting courtesy visit to Mrs Shepherd, without giving her any of the details of the trip to London and its outcome, and then, at her own request, boarded the carriage with Billy driving, to return to Nethergate.

'I feel more comfortable behind a horse,' she confessed to him. 'I'm sure motor cars will become more and more popular, but I can't see them taking over from horses, can you?'

Billy shut the door on her and grinned. 'Oh, you mark my words, Miss, motor cars is only the beginning. I reckon everything will be on four wheels soon enough.'

'Yes, and women will get the vote,' Dorinda said

grumpily to herself as the carriage began to roll down the drive.

Billy drove the carriage to Victoria Place and stopped at the top of the slope down to The Alexandria. Dorinda alighted with his help.

'Thank you, Billy.' Dorinda looked down and saw that the front door of the building was propped open. 'Will you wait until I see if there's a message to carry back to Lady Anderson?'

She went down the slope and was met by an agitated Maude.

'Oh, Dolly – you'll never guess!'

'What?' Dorinda came to an abrupt halt. 'What now?'

'Aramantha's disappeared!'

Thoughts crashed together in Dorinda's head. For a moment she was incapable of speech.

'We didn't know what to do, so we sent for Fred Fowler and he's sent for the Inspector,' Maude went on. 'He hasn't arrived yet.'

'When did this happen?' asked Dorinda.

'Yesterday. We think it was yesterday.'

'What do you mean? You think?'

'Oh, Dolly, I'm so confused.' Maude put a shaky hand to her head. 'And why are you here? We thought you were coming back tomorrow?'

'Here,' said Dorinda. 'Take my valise inside and I'll be with you in a minute. I've got to tell Ivy.'

She almost ran up the slope.

'Billy, will you tell Lady Anderson that Aramantha has gone missing? I shall try and send another message as soon as I have news.'

'Aramantha, miss? Surely.' Billy looked interested. 'Nothing else?'

'No – and thank you, Billy.'

She watched the carriage turn awkwardly and ran back down the slope.

112

'Now,' she said ushering Maude into her office. 'From the beginning.'

Maude sank down on the chair in front of the desk. 'Yesterday we decided to open in the afternoon with an old Serenaders set. We told them all you'd had to go to London and only Aramantha asked why. So Will said it was to do with Velda's murder. They were all interested, you know the way they are, but we didn't say anything else, and the girls were happy enough to learn the set. We kept in some of the songs we do now, but not the fairy one, of course.'

'How did it go?' asked Dorinda, interested in spite of the situation.

'Quite well. The audience were a bit surprised, and Mickey Bennett turned up and accused us of pinching his material, but Will sorted him out. And then when we was getting ready for the evening show, Maisie comes dashing down to the front and says Aramantha hasn't turned up.'

'Who last saw her?' asked Dorinda.

'All the girls. They went out to get something to eat, and nobody remembers her going off anywhere.'

'So what did you do?'

'Went on, same as before. She didn't have no solos in the Serenaders set, so it wasn't too bad. So after the show Will and Ted and Algy all went back to Aramantha's digs – you know she's in the same digs as Phoebe?'

'Yes – go on,' said Dorinda impatiently.

'And she wasn't there. But all her togs was.' Maude put her hand to her heart. 'Gawd, it's upset me that much.'

'So what did Will do then?'

'He went straight and woke Fred Fowler up. And Fred said he couldn't do nothing last night, but he got straight on his bike this morning and rode all the way to Deal.'

'Oh, how ridiculous!' said Dorinda. 'Why couldn't he send a telegraph?'

'Oh, I don't know. But for all I know the Inspector's

113

over at the lodgings now. Fred come down here when he got back from Deal. Poor bugger.' Maude shook her head. 'Worn out, he was.'

'Oh, lord.' Dorinda put her head in her hands.

'So why are you back already?'

'It's quite a story,' said Dorinda, looking up. 'Where's Will?'

'At the back rehearsing with all the others. I'll go and get him.'

When Will and Maude returned, Dorinda told them the story she and Ivy had learnt from Ada the previous evening.

'And so this morning we brought Ada down to The Place and she was going to have a look at Aramantha and see if it really was this Edith.' Dorinda shook her head. 'When Aramantha heard I'd gone to London I'm sure she realised that we would find out who she was and she's run away.'

'I can't believe it.' Maude shook her own head in turn. 'Why didn't they recognise each other?'

'I think Ivy had the right of it,' said Dorinda. 'Martha and Edith – or Velda and Aramantha – split up after the business at the Britannia. I suppose they both thought they'd better not give each other away.'

'And she reckons Aramantha – or whoever she is – killed Velda? To stop her talking?' said Will.

'That's what she thinks, yes.' Dorinda squinted into the distance, remembering. 'Velda stayed behind that night, didn't she? She was worried about the woman and the necklace business. Do you think she might have tackled Aramantha about that? Perhaps she really had turned over a new leaf and thought Aramantha was up to her old tricks?'

'I liked Velda,' said Maude, 'and I never liked Aramantha. I can believe that. We must tell the inspector.'

'I suspect Inspector Malkin will think I had something

114

to do with it whatever we say,' said Dorinda with a sigh. 'We'd better go and tell the others what's been going on.'

Dorinda had barely got started on her tale, seated on the stage surrounded by her company, when Inspector Malkin himself strode down towards them, followed by Constable Fowler and an uncomfortable looking sergeant.

'Well, well, well. And what have you done with this one, Miss Alexander?' The small shrewd eyes pierced Dorinda's own. 'What did *she* know about your past, hey?'

Dorinda gasped. 'What?'

'Where did you run off to yesterday? Hide her body, did you?'

There was a loud burst of outrage from the entire company. Will held up his hand and stepped right in front of the inspector.

'Miss Alexander went to London with Lady Anderson yesterday and returned only an hour ago. Inspector Colyer knew she was going. And Miss Giles – '

'Who?' interrupted Malkin.

'Aramantha Giles. She was with us for the whole of the afternoon show here. And I'm afraid I resent your questions to Miss Dorinda.'

'Resent away, Beddowes. I'm here to do a job, and you ain't got no lords and ladies to hide behind today. I say this woman comes right back to the station with me now.'

'And,' came a voice from the back of the hall, 'I say she doesn't.'

Chapter Sixteen

Jack Colyer strolled down to join Malkin in front of the stage.

'What is the matter with you?' he asked in a conversational tone. 'What have you got against Miss Alexander, who seems to me to be a very industrious, independent young woman of impeccable character?'

Dorinda felt her insides squeeze together and she swallowed hard, avoiding Maude's eyes, which she felt were fixed on her.

'I say there's something not right about that business with the necklace and those Shepherds,' said Malkin, 'and I'm going to get to the bottom of it.'

'I thought Sir Frederick and Lady Anderson had already proved there was nothing wrong?' said Colyer.

'They were covering up,' said Malkin through gritted teeth, 'and I intend to prove it, Sir or no Sir.'

'Good luck with that,' said Colyer, sounding amused. 'Meanwhile, I believe Miss Alexander has some information for us concerning both young ladies.'

Dorinda, Maude, Will and Malkin all looked at him in surprise.

'How do you know?' asked Malkin, voicing the question in all their minds.

'Lady Anderson is a very forward thinking woman, and sent me a telegraph only an hour ago.'

'How did she know where to find you?' asked Malkin suspiciously.

Colyer raised his eyebrows. 'Why, she sent it to your police station, of course. By which time you had left, but one of your sensible constables knew where I was and came and found me. You know, you really ought to have a telephone installed in your police station.'

'Tell that to the Chief Constable,' muttered Malkin.

'And now, it seems, something else has occurred?' Colyer looked brightly round the company, and finally fixed on Dorinda. 'Miss Alexander? Shall we go and sit down and you can tell me all about it?'

'Will, Maude, will you tell the others the story? I'll take the inspector – the inspectors – into the office.' Dorinda slid inelegantly off the stage, reluctantly accepting Colyer's hand.

'I'll bring tea,' said Maude, bustling off to the little stove at the back of the stage.

'Now, Miss Alexander.' Jack Colyer took the seat opposite the desk, leaving Malkin to hover impotently in the background.

Once more, Dorinda repeated the story of the trip to London and the discovery of Aramantha's flight. She also repeated Ivy's theory that Aramantha had killed Velda.

'Rubbish!' burst out Malkin.

'It doesn't seem likely,' said Colyer, looking dubious. 'Martha was strangled.'

'So you knew who she was all along,' said Dorinda. 'And all about her career?'

'Yes. I told you we were aware of her. After the Britannia she went to ground. We never knew the name of her partner, and although we had this one complaint, none of her victims had ever seen her.'

'So there had been other complaints?'

'Oh, yes, but under the circumstances the gentlemen made no formal accusations, so the various police forces throughout the country had no real evidence.'

'But you knew where she lived,' said Dorinda accusingly.

'That was a piece of luck.' Colyer smiled

117

reminiscently. 'She was seen in company with one of London's most – well, let us say a villain. A well-dressed villain. We were of the opinion that they were working together. When she came down here we followed.'

'And you thought she was up to no good here?'

'It seemed a safe conclusion. And her murder did nothing to dispel that.'

Dorinda stared at her desk deep in thought.

'Nothing to do with London,' blustered Malkin. 'There was something going on with this woman here. I know that. Never got to the bottom of it.'

'Oh, please,' sighed Dorinda, 'don't be ridiculous. I would hardly be conducting a business here in full view of police and public alike if I had a criminal past. Just concentrate on finding Aramantha Giles and Velda Turner's murderer.'

Malkin's undoubted outburst was fortunately stopped by Maude's entrance with a battered tin tray containing three cups. She slid as unobtrusively as possible back out of the door as soon as the cups were on the desk.

'It certainly looks as though the murder and this disappearance are connected,' said Colyer, politely handing a cup to his colleague. 'Don't you agree, Malkin?'

Malkin muttered indistinguishably.

'What should we do next, do you think?' Colyer persisted. Dorinda was aware that he was deliberately annoying the other inspector, and while she didn't like the man, she felt this was unnecessary.

'Please, just find Aramantha, or Edith. I can't help feeling she might be in danger.'

'You don't think she's run away?' asked Colyer.

'I think she might have done,' said Dorinda judiciously, 'because she knew if Ivy and I went to London we might learn something about her. She knew we were going to ask Ivy's sister who worked at the Britannia. But it's who she might have run to that worries me.'

118

'Why?' Malkin was frowning.

'Someone killed Velda, and I don't think it was Aramantha. So someone might want to keep her quiet.'

'About what?' asked Colyer.

'She might know what it was Velda was doing down here. I know they didn't appear to recognise each other, but they might have met in secret.' Dorinda sighed again. 'Oh, I don't know. It's all too much for me.'

Colyer and Malkin exchanged looks.

'Very well,' said Malkin, placing his empty cup on the desk. 'Shall we go and talk to these people, Colyer? See what they remember about this Aramantha person yesterday?'

Colyer smiled. 'Indeed we will, Malkin. Miss Dorinda – we shall speak again soon, no doubt. Thank you for the tea.'

Dorinda leant back in her chair and closed her eyes. She had spoken the truth. It was indeed too much for her.

Maude cautiously opened the door.

'They're talking to the girls,' she reported. 'I don't know what you did to that Malkin but he's calmed down.'

'I don't know either. But I *am* worried about Aramantha.'

'Worried?' Maude's eyebrows went up. 'If she killed Velda – '

'But I don't think she did. I think there's more behind this. I don't think it's anything to do with their career in London or other parts of the country. I think Malkin's right when he says the reasons are here.'

'In that case, we were right in the first place. It's to do with you after all. Or The Alexandria.' Maude folded her arms under her bust and looked portentous.

Dorinda nodded. 'I keep remembering the wrecked office and the woman with the necklace. Will said that must have something to do with me, didn't he? And it seems such a coincidence that Velda was murdered just after that.'

Maude shook her head. 'Well, now we've got to decide if we're going on with the show this afternoon. There are people out there, and we're open in half an hour.'

Dorinda stood up. 'Let's go and ask the inspectors if we can go on. I'd just like to get back to normal.'

The inspectors gave their consent to the afternoon show, and the company rushed to don their silver Serenaders costumes. Dorinda, three quarters of an hour later, took her place, a little shakily, at the piano, and the performance began, albeit rather raggedly. The police presence quietly evaporated and by the time the performance was over Dorinda was able to sit down in her office, pull off her hat and try to relax.

She had barely been there five minutes when the office door opened and Ivy and Ada walked in.

'What's all this then?' said Ivy. 'Edith-Aramantha gone missing? See, I told you I was right.'

'I don't think so,' said Dorinda. 'I think she might be in danger.'

'Danger? Why?'

'I'm not sure, but I am beginning to wonder...' Dorinda gazed out of the window. 'I've got an idea.'

'Come on, let's have it,' said Ivy.

'No ... I have to do this on my own. I'm going to pay a visit this afternoon.' Dorinda stood up. 'I've got time before tonight's performance. Now I'm going to change.'

Frustrated, Ivy and Ada nevertheless helped Dorinda into her flannel skirt and white blouse. Ada achieved a respectable pompadour and helped Dorinda pin her hat on top.

'Now don't follow me,' said Dorinda, preparing to leave, 'and don't say anything to Maude and Will, except to tell them I'll be back as soon as possible.'

She walked swiftly up the slope and turned towards the town. Inside, she felt almost physically sick, but now the pieces were beginning to fit together, even if most of the jigsaw was speculative. There was only one person who hated her this much, and she had to find out if she was right.

After ten minutes, she arrived at a clean little house in one of the back streets of Nethergate. Taking a deep breath, she knocked on the front door.

'Miss Alexander!' The small man who opened the door looked positively frightened. His bald head shone, his faded blue eyes watered.

'Mr Cooper.' Dorinda smiled grimly. 'How are you?'

'Miss Alexander! You haven't come – oh, dear.' He fumbled with a pair of eyeglasses and struggled to put them on.

'No,' said Dorinda. 'I haven't come to take Colin away. But I wanted to ask you if anyone else has come to ask the same thing?'

Albert Cooper's face became suffused with unlovely purple. 'I – um – I – we...'

'They have, then?' said Dorinda, her stomach seeming to turn over with fear.

'How clever of you my dear.' The voice issued from within the little house. 'You'd better let her in, Cooper.'

Dorinda stepped inside the dark little hall and immediately came face to face with a white faced Aramantha Giles, her eyes wide with fear. And from behind her appeared the stocky, pompous figure of Mr Earnest Shepherd.

Chapter Seventeen

Dorinda was aware of Albert Cooper gibbering behind her.

'Shut the door, Cooper.' Shepherd gestured to a room on his right. 'In there.'

Dorinda, heart thumping, entered the room. Heavy drapes obscured the window, and furniture too large for the tiny room filled the space. Over in the corner stood a drab woman clutching a very small boy in her arms.

She felt rather than saw Aramantha enter behind her. Earnest Shepherd herded them into the centre of the room. She turned to face him, avoiding with difficulty a chenille covered table.

'It was you, then?' she asked, trying to keep her voice steady.

The piggy eyes regarded her malevolently. 'What was?'

'You murdered Velda Turner.'

'Why should I have done that?'

Dorinda shook her head. 'I haven't worked that out yet.'

'But you have come here.' His breathing was laboured. So he wasn't as calm as he pretended, thought Dorinda. 'Why was that?'

'Someone has been trying to damage my business and ruin my reputation. The only person I could think of was you.'

Shepherd's face twisted. 'Business! Layabouts and vagabonds. And all paid for by my esteemed father-in-law.'

Dorinda raised her chin. 'To try and repair the damage you had done to me and your own family.'

He raised his hand to her, but Aramantha stepped between them and received the full force of the blow on the side of her head. She staggered into Dorinda, and the little boy began wailing.

'Shut him up,' barked Shepherd. He turned back to Dorinda. 'And now he's coming with me.'

The woman began to weep and Albert Cooper to protest.

'He comes with me and none of you will say anything about me to the police or to anyone if you want to see him alive again.' Shepherd reached across to the woman, but Dorinda got in the way.

'I won't let you take him!' she shouted. 'He may be your son, but I am his mother.'

'And that's why you came here today. I said you were clever. He is the only thing I could take from you that would really break you isn't he? I knew it would bring you, and I can hurt you as you hurt me.'

Dorinda gasped. 'I hurt *you*? When you took me by force and brought shame on your family? When you had me falsely accused of stealing the diamonds?'

'And my family banished me!' he snarled. 'My sons and daughters denied me, my business ruined? You deserve nothing but life in the gutter.' Once again he reached for the boy, and once again Aramantha tried to prevent him. This time she was sent sprawling and hit her head on the table and slid unconscious to the floor. By this time both the boy and the woman were wailing even louder, Albert Cooper was still protesting and Dorinda, trying to step over Aramantha's body, was trying to hold Shepherd back.

'Stop!'

A new voice bellowed across the noise and indeed,

stopped it. Dorinda paused and looked round at Inspector Malkin and Shepherd took the opportunity to grab the boy.

'He's mine,' he hissed.

Inspector Malkin raised an eyebrow. 'Really, sir? Now I thought this here Mr and Mrs Cooper were his lawful parents. Isn't that right, Miss Alexander?'

Dorinda, legs suddenly unable to hold her, sank down on the little table. She nodded.

'And now, who's that down there? Oh, look – it's Miss Giles that we've been looking for. I wonder how she came to be here. Now sir.' Malkin moved surprisingly easily through the obstacle course that was the sitting room, gently removed the little boy from Shepherd's arms and gave him back to his mother. 'If you'll just come along with me.' He took Shepherd's arm. 'Come along, now.'

Shepherd began to struggle and swear just as Constable Fowler and Malkin's silent sergeant appeared in the doorway and put Albert Cooper aside. Dorinda tried to shield Aramantha as Malkin propelled his captive across the room, but was unable to prevent a vicious kick landing in the girl's ribs.

Malkin looked over his shoulder and to her surprise, grinned at Dorinda. 'You'll be all right now, Miss.'

Dorinda gaped at him, just as another figure took his place.

'All right, Dorinda?' asked Jack Colyer. 'We'd better get this young lady seen to, hadn't we?' And he bent down to Aramantha.

Dorinda could hardly keep track of the events that followed. Two more constables appeared and lifted Aramantha tenderly into a carriage, Albert and Mrs Cooper were calmed down with tea made by Maude, who arrived with Ivy and Ada in tow, and little Colin burrowed into his mother's arms and stopped crying.

'When did Shepherd arrive?' Colyer asked Albert Cooper.

'This morning, with the other young lady. He said he was waiting for Miss Alexander. We didn't know what to do. He wouldn't let us leave.'

'He didn't tell you why he wanted to see Miss Alexander?'

'No, but he seemed sure she would come.'

'And of course, she did.' Colyer turned a wry grin on Dorinda. 'Having worked it all out. Good job Maude and Ivy took a guess as to where you'd gone.'

'That man,' Ada all but whispered.

They all turned to her. 'Shepherd?' said Colyer.

'Is that his name?' She looked at Dorinda.

'Yes,' said Ivy, Dorinda and Maude together.

'He's the one who reported Martha and Edith to Crauford.'

'Ah!' Light dawned on all three women. For a minute Colyer looked confused. Dorinda explained.

'It's the link. Shepherd was bilked by the pair of them working together, and trailed them back to their lodgings, only we didn't know it was Shepherd. He must have kept in touch with them. But I don't know exactly why he brought them here.'

'Perhaps Miss Giles will be able to tell us when she regains consciousness,' said Colyer. 'And now I think we shall leave Mr and Mrs Cooper to recover from a nasty experience. Your carriage is outside is it not, Lady Anderson?'

'No, I've got the motor car.' Ivy looked round the company doubtfully. 'I don't think I'll get us all in.'

'I shall take Miss Alexander back in my carriage,' said Colyer, and Dorinda's heart sank.

They bade farewell to Mr and Mrs Cooper, and Dorinda placed a kiss on little Colin's cheek and a coin in his chubby hand. Ivy saw a nervous Ada and Maude into the motor car, Billy saluted Dorinda, and Colyer ushered her into the gig that stood waiting a little way along the

125

street.

'How did you know where to find me?' she asked as the gig began to move.

'I told you – Ivy and Maude guessed as soon as you said you were paying a call. I happened to turn up at the right time and they told me. They were just preparing to come after you on their own, but I persuaded them to wait for reinforcements. Luckily, Malkin hadn't returned to Deal and was only too pleased to take the lead in a possible arrest.'

'Ah.' Dorinda stared at her clasped hands, wondering where this conversation was going, and hoping it might stop there. It didn't.

'And now perhaps you'll tell me why you went there and what exactly happened three years ago?'

Dorinda tuned an imploring gaze on him. 'Do I have to?'

'I think so. You've been keeping back information which might have helped us find this man sooner – and saved Miss Giles from injury.'

Dorinda bowed her head.

'Very well.' She sighed and looked up and out of the window.

'Three years ago I was working for Mr and Mrs Shepherd as a governess to their daughter Julia. We lived in a house in Kensington, London. That summer, Mrs Shepherd's father, Sir Frederick, took a house here in Nethergate, on Cliff Terrace, for the summer for us all. The boys – they have two – were to join us in the holidays and Mr Shepherd at weekends.'

Colyer nodded. 'As many families did.'

'But then,' Dorinda coloured, 'Mr Shepherd began to pester me. Ivy, May and Ellen tried to shield me as much as they could, and at weekends we all came down to the sands to watch the Pierrots – Will's Wanderers – as often as we could. I actually got very friendly with their bottler,

Peter Prince.'

She paused and looked down again at her lap. 'Then it got worse. One Saturday Mr Shepherd followed Ivy and me to the beach and watched me talking to Peter. That night he came to my room and...' she stopped. Colyer reached over and took one of her hands.

'I couldn't cry out, partly because he put one hand across my mouth and besides, Julia was asleep in the next room. He was vicious. The next day I ran away to the Pierrots. I didn't actually tell them what had happened, but it wasn't difficult to work out. We knew he would come after me, so Maude ran me up a costume and I bundled my hair under a hat. They had a piano on wheels, and as I could play, for two days I became their pianist. Ivy came down to ask them if they'd seen me, and we told her the truth. She went back and told May and Ellen.

'Then came the business of the necklace. Sir Frederick had been pestering Ivy to marry him for some time, but she, being very aware of the differences between them, refused. But Mrs Shepherd, who was scared of her husband for good reason, as we found out later, said she thought it would be a very good thing, and finally Ivy accepted. Which was when Sir Fred took the diamonds back from Mrs Shepherd.'

'Why didn't she tell Mr Shepherd?' asked Colyer.

'He didn't ask. We still don't know why he was going through her jewel case – she should have kept the diamonds somewhere safer – but he found the necklace missing and decided it was a perfect way to have his revenge on me. He marched straight down to the Wanderers' pitch and demanded to know where I was. You know the rest. He was humiliated.'

'Where did you go?'

'I stayed with Will and Maude at first. Mrs Shepherd begged me to go back, but I couldn't. I taught a few piano lessons until it was obvious I...' she stopped and swallowed.

'That little Colin was on the way?' suggested Colyer gently.

She nodded. 'Then Ivy told Sir Frederick the whole story. By this time they were all back in London, and Sir Fred took Mrs Shepherd and all her household into his own. Mr Shepherd was left on his own in the London house and Sir Frederick let it be known that he had taken Mrs Shepherd into his protection. Mr Shepherd's business began to fall off, and I gather he was snubbed by many of his own circle.'

'I can see why he wanted revenge,' said Colyer.

'Yes, which is why I eventually guessed what had happened.' She shrugged. 'The rest of the story is simple. Sir Frederick opened Anderson Place, took the family down there and eventually Ivy and Mrs Shepherd persuaded me to go there, too, for – for the rest of...

'Yes.' Colyer nodded.

'Then we – or Sir Fred – found Mr and Mrs Cooper, whom he had known as servants, and they took Colin.' Dorinda clenched her hands.

'Hard. But sensible,' said Colyer. She nodded.

'Then, because Will had gone up to join a big company in the north-east, I took over and we became the Silver Serenaders the next summer. We did so well I was able to buy a pitch for the next season, then Sir Frederick persuaded me to let him fund the building of The Alexandria during last winter. This is our first year as a proper concert party.'

They fell silent as the gig pulled up behind Ivy's motor car on Victoria Place.

'Now we need Miss Giles' account of things,' said Colyer, and pressed Dorinda's hand. 'Don't worry. We will not let this story spread. This is what you were afraid of, isn't it? That your son's existence would become known?'

'My reputation would be ruined. Can you imagine?'

128

Dorinda turned to him. 'I would have been spurned, my business would have been in ruins, too.'

He shook his head. 'It wasn't your fault.'

'But society doesn't see it like that. The woman is always blamed.'

Colyer couldn't argue with that. Instead, he jumped down from the gig, then helped her down.

'Let us see if Miss Aramantha has anything to tell us,' he said.

'Is she here?' Dorinda was surprised.

'I told them to bring her here rather than her own digs. And certainly not the police station. Let us go and see, shall we?'

Chapter Eighteen

Aramantha Giles, whey-faced, lay on an improvised couch in the ladies dressing room, a bandage round her head with Maude, Ivy and Ada in attendance.

She shrank back when she saw Dorinda and Colyer. Dorinda went forward and knelt by her side.

'Don't worry, Aramantha – or should I call you Edith?'

Aramantha's eyes filled with tears. 'I'm so sorry, Miss Dolly.'

'Why don't you tell us what happened? Right from the beginning? Don't mind the inspector. He just wants to know.'

Colyer and Dorinda were both provided with stools as Aramantha haltingly began her story.

'Martha and me, we met Shepherd while we was at the Britannia.' The pale face became tinged with pink.

'We know all about that.' Dorinda indicated Ada hovering in the background.

'Gawd, Ada! I didn't recognize you!'

Ada gave a small deprecating smile.

'Well, you know all about that. But after, 'e kept in touch. 'E knew all about us, see, so 'e thought 'e could do what 'e liked with us. And 'e used us both. For all sorts of things.' She cast a surreptitious glance at Colyer. 'Anyway, Martha, she managed to break away. She said the police knew who we were and they'd come knocking sooner or later.'

'We knew her, but not you,' said Colyer. 'You, in fact, were quite safe.'

'Wouldn't yer know it!' said Aramantha. 'Anyway, then Shepherd says 'e 'as a job for me one day when I says you'd come and 'ired me for The Alexandria. 'E knew 'oo you were, see.'

'And you were to try and ruin the business?' said Dorinda.

More colour came into Aramantha's cheeks. 'Yes. Only, I liked it 'ere, see? I didn't want to do it. I was good at me job, wasn't I?'

'You were.' Dorinda patted her hand. 'So what happened next?'

'Then Martha turned up. I was that shocked. We didn't let on like, that we knew each other, but we 'ad quiet words. She'd actually found out from Shepherd what 'e was doing, and she wanted to stop it.' She grasped Dorinda's hand. 'It wasn't me did the office – it was 'im. And the woman with the necklace. See, I wasn't being quick enough, so 'e come down himself. And Martha – she was that upset. And she made me tell 'er where I was meeting 'im that night.' She shrugged. 'And I did.'

'So he murdered her,' said Colyer. 'What did you do then?'

'Kept me 'ead down.' Aramantha made a face. 'Till yesterday. I knew if you'd gone up to London you were onto me and Martha. Or you would be.' She grinned wanly at Ada. 'And I was right, wasn't I?'

'Did you meet him?' asked Dorinda.

''E was watching this place the whole time. 'E'd seen you leave in the motor car, and when I come out after the show, 'e caught me up on the prom and carted me off to 'is 'ouse.'

'Where?' asked Dorinda.

'Up there.' Aramantha pointed vaguely. 'Cliff Terrace.'

'The old house, of course,' breathed Dorinda.

''E kept me locked in there till this morning, when he dragged me up to them Coopers.' She looked up at

Dorinda. 'Was 'e right? Was that kid yours?' Dorinda nodded. 'Shepherd's a right bastard, ain't 'e?'

Colyer stood up. 'That's all we need, Miss Giles.' He smiled crookedly down at her. 'Is that what we call you?'

She grinned cautiously back. 'Better than Edith Small. What yer going to do with me?'

Colyer looked at Dorinda. 'Make you stay and finish the season?'

Aramantha gaped. Dorinda smiled.

'Yes, a fitting punishment, I think. And I haven't forgotten that you tried to protect me from Shepherd. Once you're well, of course. Perhaps a little holiday first.'

'You come back home with me, love,' said Ivy. 'We got plenty of room, haven't we, Ada? And we've looked after the sick before, eh, Doll?' She winked at Dorinda.

Colyer guided Dorinda back to her office and shut the door behind them.

'Nice of you to have her back,' he said perching on the edge of her desk.

'Nice of you to suggest it,' countered Dorinda.

'And what now, Miss Alexander?'

Dorinda looked out of the window. 'I carry on. I try and get over all this. The company will help me. Will I have to go to the trial? He will go to trial?'

'I'm afraid you and Aramantha will have to give evidence. Oh, not,' he said seeing her flinch, 'about anything that happened three years ago. We will keep it simple. He won't be allowed to say anything.'

'Oh.' Dorinda subsided into her chair, avoiding his eyes.

'Dorinda.' He stood up, came round the desk and pulled her out of the chair. 'Listen to me. You are not ruined, only in your own eyes. Mrs Shepherd, Sir Frederick and Ivy don't consider you ruined, do they? Neither do Maude and Will, and they know all about it, too.'

'I can never marry,' Dorinda fixed her eyes over his left shoulder.

He shrugged. 'That, of course, is up to you. But you should not deny yourself the opportunities available to a good looking young woman.' He gave her a little shake. 'Start to live, Dorinda.'

'I do!' she said, affronted. 'I've got my business, and as you've just said, my friends.'

He gave her a quizzical look. 'Are you being deliberately blind?'

'I don't think so,' said Dorinda, going pink.

He sighed and let her go. 'Are you going to allow what happened to blight your life?'

'I don't know what you mean.' Dorinda sat down again and dropped her eyes to the desk. 'I have just said, I have my work and my friends.' She looked up. 'And I believe I shall devote a little more time to trying to change society's attitude to women.'

Colyer's face darkened. 'A dangerous occupation.'

Dorinda leant back in her chair and looked up at him. 'I thought you were different. Do you really believe women are inferior to men?'

'I believe *we* are different.' Colyer's eyes slid from hers.

'Of course we are. But are our brains so dissimilar? Would you not agree I am making a success of my business? Do you not think I may progress even further?'

Colyer's eyes returned to her face. 'I believe you will do whatever you want. But there are some things women are just not fitted to do.'

'Like having the vote?'

'Joining the police force, for instance. Investigating crimes.'

Dorinda looked thoughtfully at her hands. 'Really. Ivy and I wasted our time in London, I suppose?'

'Of course not.' Colyer made a sound of exasperation and took a turn around the room.

'I'm extremely glad about that.' Dorinda stood up and held out a hand. 'Thank you for your help and your discretion, Inspector Colyer. I greatly appreciate it. I don't expect we shall see you again.'

Looking surprised, Colyer came forward and took her hand. 'But I shall see you at the trial.'

'Of course.' Dorinda inclined her head. 'But it isn't likely that our paths will cross after that.'

'Unless you become involved with Mrs Pankhurst,' said Colyer.

'Oh, I doubt that,' said Dorinda, withdrawing her hand. 'Goodbye, Inspector Colyer.'

He hesitated. Then, 'Goodbye – Dorinda.' He took her hand and dropped a kiss on the back before leaving the room.

Dorinda stared at the closed door and wondered why her heart was beating rather fast. And why she felt such an almost painful sense of loss. She sat down and put her head in her hands.

'Don't worry, lovie.' Maude's arm was round her shoulders, her free hand pushing a clean handkerchief into Dorinda's own. 'It's all been a bit much, today, hasn't it?'

Dorinda lifted her head and gave Maude a drowned smile. 'It has a bit.'

Maude nodded wisely. 'And he'll be back.'

'Back? Who?' Dorinda eyes widened.

'Your Inspector Colyer.' Maude smiled and patted her shoulder. 'He won't take no for an answer.'

'I don't know what you mean.' Dorinda looked away.

'You don't think you do,' said Maude. 'Now, I'm going to make us some more tea. You pull yourself together.'

Dorinda sat for a long time alone in her office. She thought about many things – Velda Turner, Aramantha

Giles, Ivy, Maude and Will and – Inspector Colyer. Women's Suffrage and the investigation of crimes. And wondered …

The End

Á

For more information about
Lesley Cookman
and other **Accent Press** titles

please visit

www.accentpress.co.uk

45459434R00082

Printed in Poland
by Amazon Fulfillment
Poland Sp. z o.o., Wrocław